ALONE IN THE HOUSE?

The room was round and stuck off the side of the house. It held only the black-covered table and two chairs.

Herculeah noticed now that one of the chairs—the velvet chair that Madame Rosa always sat in—had been overturned.

She turned to go. Glancing down, she saw something sticking out from under the black cloth that was draped over the table.

It was a black, booted foot—a small one. The frayed shoelaces were tied neatly at the ankle.

Madame Rosa wore boots like this.

A feeling of nausea washed over Herculeah like a wave. She could barely stand. Her knees began to tremble.

She reached out one unsteady hand and drew back the worn velvet cloth....

"Byars grips the reader from the first sentence and doesn't let go until Herculeah solves the case."

—*The Horn Book*

BOOKS BY BETSY BYARS

The Herculeah Jones Mysteries:
The Dark Stairs
Tarot Says Beware
Dead Letter
Death's Door
Disappearing Acts
King of Murder

The Bingo Brown books:
Bingo Brown, Gypsy Lover
Bingo Brown and the Language of Love
Bingo Brown's Guide to Romance
The Burning Questions of Bingo Brown

Other titles:
After the Goat Man
The Cartoonist
The Computer Nut
Cracker Jackson
The Cybil War
The 18th Emergency
The Glory Girl
The House of Wings
McMummy
The Midnight Fox
The Summer of the Swans
Trouble River
The TV Kid

XIII

A HERCULEAH JONES MYSTERY

TAROT SAYS BEWARE

BY BETSY BYARS

SLEUTH
PUFFIN

PUFFIN BOOKS
Published by the Penguin Group
Penguin Young Readers Group, 345 Hudson Street, New York, New York 10014, U.S.A.
Penguin Group (Canada), 90 Eglinton Avenue East, Suite 700, Toronto, Ontario,
Canada M4P 2Y3 (a division of Pearson Penguin Canada Inc.)
Penguin Books Ltd, 80 Strand, London WC2R 0RL, England
Penguin Ireland, 25 St Stephen's Green, Dublin 2, Ireland (a division of Penguin Books Ltd)
Penguin Group (Australia), 250 Camberwell Road, Camberwell, Victoria 3124, Australia
(a division of Pearson Australia Group Pty Ltd)
Penguin Books India Pvt Ltd, 11 Community Centre, Panchsheel Park, New Delhi - 110 017, India
Penguin Group (NZ), Cnr Airborne and Rosedale Roads, Albany, Auckland 1310, New Zealand
(a division of Pearson New Zealand Ltd)
Penguin Books (South Africa) (Pty) Ltd, 24 Sturdee Avenue, Rosebank,
Johannesburg 2196, South Africa

Registered Offices: Penguin Books Ltd, 80 Strand, London WC2R 0RL, England

First published in the United States of America by Viking,
a division of Penguin Books USA Inc., 1995
Published by Puffin Books, 1997
This edition published by Puffin Books, a division of Penguin Young Readers Group, 2006

1 3 5 7 9 10 8 6 4 2

THE LIBRARY OF CONGRESS HAS CATALOGED THE VIKING EDITION AS FOLLOWS:
Byars, Betsy Cromer.
Tarot says beware / by Betsy Byars. p. cm.—(A Herculeah Jones mystery)
Summary: Herculeah Jones and her bumbling pal, Meat,
investigate the murder of a palm reader.
ISBN: 0-670-85575-8
[1. Mystery and detective stories.] I. Title. II. Series.
PZ7.B9836Tar 1995 [Fic]—dc20 95-12334 CIP AC

Puffin Books ISBN 0-14-240593-0

Printed in the United States of America

CONTENTS

1. A Warning from Tarot   1
2. Danger on the Stairs   10
3. Death in the Parlor   16
4. A Cry for Help   22
5. A Ring for Madame Rosa   26
6. Scene of the Crime   34
7. Fingerprints   38
8. The Mime   44
9. A Suspect   50
10. A Key at Midnight   56
11. The Shadow   61
12. Killer Puppets   68
13. Which Witch   73
14. Fogging Out   77
15. Walk-ins Unwelcome   83
16. Footsteps   87
17. Voodoo Dolls and All That Jazz   92
18. Foot Nightmares   97
19. The Other Half of the Picture   104
20. Dear Abby   109
21. Meat and Mime   113

Contents

22. Madame Rosa Calls   119

23. The Black Robe   125

24. The Knife   130

25. Weapon of Choice   137

26. Living Up to Herculeah   141

27. Herculeah and the Golden Fleece   147

1

A WARNING FROM TAROT

Herculeah Jones was restless. She went to the window and looked up and down the street. Everything seemed normal, but she could not shake the feeling that something was wrong.

She went to the phone on her mother's desk. She dialed her friend Meat's number. There was no answer. She went back to the window.

This time her eyes narrowed at something she saw down the street—a flicker of motion. The binoculars were on the end table. Herculeah picked them up and lifted them to her face. She adjusted the lens. She leaned forward in her intensity.

She noticed three things:

1. The door to Madame Rosa's house was open.
2. Madame Rosa's parrot had flown outside and was now perched on one of the porch rockers.
3. Her hair was beginning to frizzle.

She thought, Now I know something's wrong. Her hair always did this when there was danger. Meat had once called it "radar hair," and she had smiled. Herculeah wasn't smiling now.

She rushed into the hall, pulling on her sweater as she ran out the door. Pausing only to check for traffic, she crossed the street.

Madame Rosa's house was the fourth one down. There was a sign in front, in the shape of an open hand, that said:

Madame Rosa
Palmist
Walk-ins Welcome

Herculeah opened the gate and paused by the sign. She often came to Madame Rosa's to feed the parrot when Madame Rosa was out of town. It alarmed her to see the parrot loose, because Madame Rosa was very particular about him. Something had to be badly wrong.

"Tarot," Herculeah said in a calm voice, not wanting to alarm the bird.

Tarot cocked his head and looked back with round eyes dulled slightly by the cold.

She glanced up at the house. "Madame Rosa, Tarot's out!" she called.

She waited, but Madame Rosa did not appear in the open doorway.

"Madame Rosa!"

Again no answer.

Slowly Herculeah started up the walk.

"It's just me, Herculeah," she told the bird. "You want to go back inside, don't you, where it's warm? I'll even feed you." The bird took a side step on the back of the rocker. "You want to go back to your perch? Then don't fly off, Tarot."

The bird lifted his wings and flapped them but didn't go anywhere.

"That's right. Don't fly off. I'm taking you back in the house. Madame Rosa, your parrot's out on the porch!"

Herculeah slipped off her sweater as she climbed the stairs. The parrot lifted his wings in another feeble flutter.

"It's just me. I feed you, remember? I'm going to help you back in the house."

In one lightning-fast move, Herculeah threw her

3

sweater around the bird. "Gotcha," she said. She felt a moment of relief because Tarot was easily startled and she could have ended up chasing him all over the neighborhood.

She carried him to the open door. She paused in the doorway.

There were no lights on inside the house. Herculeah's feeling of relief at catching the parrot so easily was replaced by a chill of dread.

"Madame Rosa?"

The parrot struggled in her arms. "It's all right, Tarot. I'll let you out in a minute."

Herculeah entered and shoved the front door shut with her shoulder. She walked into the dark living room.

The huge pieces of furniture had been in place since the house had been built seventy years ago. The velvet drapes—almost as old—were drawn against the afternoon light. Herculeah clicked on a lamp as she passed the table.

The parrot's stand had been turned over and lay across the faded and worn Persian rug.

"You must have gotten scared when your stand tipped over, huh? That's why you flew out on the porch?" she said, though she had the feeling that that was not what had happened.

She picked up the parrot's stand. There was something else wrong about the room, but she couldn't place what it was.

She unwrapped the trembling bird and placed him on his perch. He took a few steps and began to swing his head from side to side.

"Something happened in this house," Herculeah stated. "Madame Rosa would never let you go outside—not if she could have prevented it."

She turned, slowly looking into the shadows of the room. She remembered that the last time she had been here, Madame Rosa had tried to pay her for looking after Tarot.

"No," Herculeah had said. "I like feeding him. It's no trouble at all."

"I want to pay. You do me a big favor. Here, take it. Go on. Take." She held out some money.

"No. Oh, I have an idea," Herculeah had said. "Give me a reading. I want to know if I'm going to get an A on my English test tomorrow."

"I thought you didn't believe in readings," Madame Rosa said with a smile that showed her long teeth. Her dark, gray-streaked hair was held back with golden combs.

"Well, I do and I don't," Herculeah said.

"Which? You do? You don't?"

"Well, if you tell me I'm going to get an A, then I'll

probably work real hard and I will get one. So go ahead. Read the future."

She held out her hands, palms up. Madame Rosa leaned over them. Herculeah could smell the scent of herbs and foreign perfume.

Madame Rosa put her hands under Herculeah's. Her touch was light, but it seemed to offer strong support. Herculeah understood why people trusted Madame Rosa's advice.

"Ah," she said.

"What?"

"I see a very long lifeline."

"What else?"

"I see a boy who is in love with you—two boys, one dark, one fair."

"Madame Rosa, all I'm interested in right now is my English grade."

"I do see a letter—perhaps it stands for a grade. We can never be sure."

"What is the letter?"

Herculeah really did not believe in palm readings and crystal balls, yet for some reason, she felt an excitement. It was like being part of a soap opera.

"It is—" She paused. "I must look more closely."

"What letter, Madame Rosa? I'm getting serious about this."

"We cannot rush the future." Madame Rosa had

bent closer. "Ah, it is becoming clearer, clearer. It is an A. See?"

With one finger Madame Rosa drew a capital A on Herculeah's palm. Then she deftly slipped the bills on the open hand and closed Herculeah's fingers around them.

"That wasn't fair," Herculeah had said.

As she stood in the living room, she realized that was the last time she had seen Madame Rosa. She had stood right here between the parrot stand and the huge old buffet that held pictures of Madame Rosa's relatives. "All dead but one—no, I forget to count myself," she had once said. "All dead but two."

Again Herculeah felt a chill, and she pulled on her sweater. "Madame Rosa?" Where could she be?

She glanced in the small parlor where Madame Rosa gave her readings. The round table in the center of the room was draped with a black cloth, and a large, gold-edged book lay open upon it. The heavy curtains were drawn in this room, too.

Herculeah moved back through the living room and into the hall. Her feeling of unease grew. The house had never been so silent, so filled with dread.

"Madame Rosa?"

She walked back into the kitchen. She smelled something burning and she went to the stove. A pot of some kind of liquid had boiled away. Perhaps, she thought, Madame Rosa had been disturbed in the middle of cooking something. Perhaps she had rushed out, leaving the front door open and . . . Herculeah's thoughts trailed off.

She turned off the burner and shifted the pot. She opened the door to the backyard and peered out. There was no one in sight.

She moved through the hall, checking the rooms on either side as she went—the downstairs bedroom, the library, the sunroom, the bathroom. All were empty.

She paused at the foot of the stairs. Again she called, "Madame Rosa?"

She glanced at the coatrack beside the door. Madame Rosa's long, black cloak hung there. Madame Rosa never went out without that cloak. Even in the summer, she wore it slung back over her shoulders. Madame Rosa had not gone out of this house.

A shiver of fear ran up Herculeah's spine. She wrapped her arms about herself.

She put her foot on the first step.

In the living room Tarot had warmed up and regained his strength. "Beware! Beware!" he screeched. "Beware" was the parrot's only word.

Herculeah had always thought this was comical. She liked it when she passed the house and Tarot screeched his warning out the window. She would pause to listen. "Beware! Beware!"

She knew that all the neighbors did not feel the same way. Some of them had complained to the police about the noise. And unsuspecting strangers walked faster when they passed by, as if they took the warning seriously.

Now it didn't seem comical at all.

Gripping the banister tightly, Herculeah started up the stairs.

2

DANGER ON THE STAIRS

Herculeah stopped at the head of the staircase. She could see her reflection in the long mirror at the end of the hall. Her hair was so frizzled that she seemed to have been electrified.

She pulled her hair back into a ponytail with her hands.

"Quit doing that. I am not in danger," she told her hair. She hoped it was true.

She breathed deeply to calm herself. "Madame Rosa?" Her voice seemed small, lost in the huge hall.

She had never been upstairs in this house before. There was a musty smell, as if the upstairs rooms had not been used in a long time. Herculeah moved down the worn carpet, opening the doors one by one.

She saw undusted objects, beds that had not been slept in for years, toilet bowls orange and dry, faded rugs. Maybe people had once occupied these rooms, but they had left nothing of themselves behind.

She paused at the front window and looked at the street below. She saw her friend Meat crossing the street to the opposite sidewalk. Meat was one of the people who crossed to avoid Tarot's cries of "Beware."

She tried to open the window to call to him. But the window had not been opened in years. She rapped on the glass. Meat kept walking.

The night before, she and Meat had talked on the phone about their English assignment. "Have you done yours yet, Meat? The assignment where we have to tell who we are in at least fifty words or more. I can't seem to get started."

"Write about how you got your name."

"Oh, I don't know."

"Or your radar hair."

"Maybe. What are you going to write?"

Meat said, "I've already started, 'My name is Meat,

and I'm fat, obese, chunky, overweight, a lard-butt, a tubbo, el blimpo— Only I'm not sure I'll be able to think of, let's see, thirty-four more words for fat."

Herculeah knew that Meat frequently said things like this so that she would tell him she never thought of him as fat—which she didn't.

This time she said, "You're getting taller. And, Meat, if you get tall enough, you'll be just right."

"How tall do I have to get?" he asked. "Ten feet? Twenty?"

"How tall was your dad?"

"You know I haven't seen him since I was five."

"Was he tall then?"

"I was five years old, Herculeah. All adults were tall."

"Ask your mom how tall your dad was. Surely she'll tell you that much."

"She goes out of the room when I even mention his name."

"Meat, you have a right to know. I looked at you through my glasses one time"—Herculeah had thick granny glasses that turned the world into a pleasant blur and allowed her to "fog out," as she called it— "and I saw you as six feet, four inches tall."

Herculeah smiled a little, remembering the conversation. She turned away from the window. At that moment she heard a noise downstairs. A footstep? The smile froze on her face.

"Madame Rosa?" It was barely a whisper.

There was no answer.

Her heart began to pound. There was someone else in the house.

"Beware! Beware!" the parrot screeched below. The parrot never said that to Madame Rosa, only when he saw a stranger. And if Tarot could see the stranger from the living room, whoever it was had to be close to the staircase.

She glanced around her. Here, at the far end of the hall, she was trapped. If someone came up the stairs, the only place she could go was into one of the musty bedrooms. Then she would really be trapped.

At the other end of the hall, her mirror image reflected her fear.

She heard another footstep in the hall below. It was louder. The stranger was coming closer.

Herculeah waited. She tried to swallow, but her throat had gone dry.

If the footsteps started up the stairs, she decided, she would . . . Would what? What?

She looked around. On the hall table, there was a huge iron candlestick. Melted wax crusted the sides. Herculeah picked it up and tested it. It was hard and long, like a twisted iron baseball bat. It would have to do.

There were no sounds from below now, but Herculeah's heart was pounding in her ears so hard that she wasn't sure she would be able to hear anything. Someone could be halfway up the stairs by now.

She peered over the banister. There was no one on the stairs. That did not bring her any real relief. The person could be just out of sight—in the hallway.

Holding the candlestick in both hands, ready to strike, she moved to the head of the stairs.

She could see no one in the hall below. "Is there anybody down there?"

She went down one step. The old stair creaked under her weight. Another step. Another.

Now she could see that the front door was open in the entrance hall. She paused.

Hadn't she closed that door when she came in? She wasn't sure. She thought she remembered shoving it shut with her shoulder, but maybe not. The whole episode was beginning to take on the confusion of a dream—no, she corrected herself, a nightmare.

She would take the rest of the steps in a rush, she decided. And if anybody was stupid enough to try and stop her, she would swing the candlestick like Dave

Justice. Then she would get out the door as fast as she could and run for her life.

She rushed down the stairs, her lips pulled back in a grimace of intensity, her hair flying out wildly behind her, the candlestick pulled back to strike.

At the bottom of the steps, she stopped. The hall was empty.

3

DEATH IN THE PARLOR

Herculeah looked around, puzzled.

"I wonder if that noise could have been the parrot," Herculeah said to herself. "Tarot could have gotten off the perch and flown into something." Her head lifted with sudden thought. "If that bird got out again . . ."

She went into the living room. The parrot was there, on his perch. "Beware! Beware!" he cried, ruffling his feathers.

Herculeah was still clutching the candlestick. She set it down on a table and flexed her fingers.

"Beware!"

"Don't worry. That is exactly what I'm going to do. I

am definitely going to beware." Herculeah wasn't sure whether she was talking to calm the parrot—or herself. "I'm going to call my mom. She's a private investigator. Or maybe I should call my dad—he's a police lieutenant. But he wouldn't take this seriously. He thinks I have way too much imagination. Now, where's the phone?"

The phone was on the buffet, half hidden by the family pictures. All the photographs were old and faded. There were no color shots of babies sitting on Santa's lap or being hugged by the Easter Bunny.

The pictures were in disarray now. Some of them had fallen and lay facedown. Herculeah dialed her home number. She began to straighten the pictures as she waited for her mother to pick up.

She looked into the old faces. Here was a young one—Madame Rosa as a girl. Herculeah looked at the pretty girl in the peasant blouse and full skirt. Amazing how much she looked like herself as an adult. That's what a big nose would do for you, Herculeah thought. Cheeks and eyes could change with age, but a nose . . .

And here was Madame Rosa with her sister. Herculeah had once asked if they were twins.

And somewhere there was a picture of Madame Rosa with a child. Herculeah had meant to ask if he was her son. She had a hard time imagining Madame Rosa as a mother.

Herculeah searched for that picture as she replaced the others. It didn't seem to be there.

On the fourth ring, the phone was answered by her mother's recorded voice, and Herculeah put down the picture she was holding. She sighed with disappointment.

"This is Mim Jones. I can't take your call right now, but you can leave a message at the beep, and I'll get back to you."

At the beep, Herculeah said, "Mom, it's me. I thought you'd be home by now. Well, I hoped so. I'm down at Madame Rosa's and, Mom, she's missing. I noticed that her front door was open and her parrot was outside—which was very strange. And her cloak's here. You know she never goes out without that.

"As soon as you get home, Mom, please come down here. I'm going to sit out on the porch and wait. I'm scared to stay in the house by myself. I can't exactly explain why, but, Mom, I just know something is terribly, terribly wrong. Please come!"

She hung up the phone and turned. She now stood at the arch that led to what Madame Rosa called her parlor.

The room was round and stuck off the side of the house. It held only the black-covered table and two chairs.

Herculeah noticed now that one of the chairs—the velvet chair that Madame Rosa always sat in—had been overturned. She went into the room to put it back where it belonged.

The chair was heavy. It was an old carved chair with a dark-red velvet seat and back. The arms of the chair were carved in the shape of lion's claws. Madame Rosa had rubbed her hands over these claws so often that the finish had been worn away.

Herculeah picked up the chair and set it beside the table. She brushed her own fingers over the smooth wood, thinking of Madame Rosa's hands.

She turned to go. Glancing down, she saw something sticking out from under the black cloth that was draped over the table.

She drew in a ragged breath. She felt suddenly dizzy, and she steadied herself with one hand on the table. She stayed like that, frozen with dread. Her heart began to pound.

It was a foot, a black, booted foot—a small one. The frayed shoelaces were tied neatly at the ankle.

Madame Rosa wore boots like this.

A feeling of nausea washed over Herculeah like a wave. She could barely stand. Her knees began to tremble. She sank down into Madame Rosa's chair. She swallowed, but something in her throat wouldn't go down.

She reached out one unsteady hand and drew back the worn velvet cloth. She gasped.

Madame Rosa lay crumpled under the table, curled on her side. One hand was flung out as if offering something to someone. The other was curved at her chest.

Her long hair had come loose from the golden combs that usually held it and hung over her face. Herculeah was glad she couldn't see Madame Rosa's expression, whatever it might be.

Herculeah's eyes drifted downward. One of Madame Rosa's hands, the fingers curved at her chest, circled the blade of a knife.

She saw the bloodstains that spread out on either side of the body like wings, darkening the pale Persian carpet. She choked on the thick scent of blood that suddenly filled her nostrils.

Herculeah began to tremble violently. She knew she shouldn't touch anything, but she had to make sure Madame Rosa was dead. She might still be alive. It was possible.

Herculeah reached for Madame Rosa's outstretched hand. She touched her fingers to the thin wrist. She waited, and the brief moment of hope faded.

There was no pulse at all. The skin was cool. The living warmth had drained from her body.

Herculeah's mind seemed to move so slowly toward

the fact of Madame Rosa's death that she wondered if it would ever catch up with her emotions. Would this slow mind ever allow her to get up, to act?

Slowly, unsteadily, she got to her feet. She rested against the table for a moment, glancing down at the closed book on the table.

Then, with tears filling her eyes, Herculeah went again to the phone.

4

A CRY FOR HELP

"Police Department, Zone Three. This is Captain Morrison. Can I help you?"

"Is Chico J-Jones there?" Herculeah said. Her teeth chattered with nervousness. "It's important. I'm Herculeah, his daughter, but I'm calling on official police business."

"Hold on."

The shock of finding Madame Rosa's body rolled over her again, like the aftershock of an earthquake. She waited tensely for her father to come on the line. The phone trembled in her hand.

The smell of the blood that had seeped onto the pale

carpet still choked her. She wondered that she hadn't noticed the smell when she first came in. Now it seemed overpowering.

She felt as if she was going to gag, and she pulled her hair across her face and inhaled the clean, familiar scent of lemon verbena shampoo.

"Hello, Chico Jones here."

"Dad?"

"Hey, how's my favorite daughter?"

"Not too good."

"Oh? Something wrong at school?"

"No."

"Your mom?"

"Mom's fine."

"Then what? Don't let's play games. I'm a busy man."

"This is no game." She swallowed. "Dad, I just found a body."

There was a silence.

"Another one?" her father asked.

"This is d-different. This is not like Dead Oaks. This is somebody I know, somebody I like. Dad, I really need help."

"Where is this body?" There was a different tone to his voice now. He was official. She could imagine him picking up a pencil, pulling that yellow legal pad toward him.

"Dad, do you remember that house down the street from Mom and me? It's a big old house with a s-sign out in front shaped like a hand? Madame Rosa—Palmist—Walk-ins Welcome. I'm sure I've told you about her. I take care of her parrot."

"Is that where you found the body? At the palmist's house?"

"Yes."

"And the body?"

"It's hers, Dad. Madame Rosa's."

She choked back a sob and took a few steps away from the room where the body lay. Again, she took a whiff of her hair.

"Where are you now?"

"I'm there. At her house. I'm in the living room. I can see her foot sticking out from under the—"

"I'm on my way," her father interrupted.

Herculeah could hear him push back his chair and get to his feet. She should feel relief, she thought, but she glanced around uneasily.

"I'm going to wait for you out on the porch. I don't feel safe at all."

"All right, but don't touch anything."

"I already have." She kept talking because suddenly she couldn't bear to let her father go. "I straightened pictures and the parrot stand and Madame Rosa's chair and a candlestick and I turned on the lamp and turned off the stove and—"

"Is there anything you didn't touch?" her father interrupted dryly.

"Yes," Herculeah said. "The knife in Madame Rosa's chest."

5

A Ring for Madame Rosa

Herculeah shook her head back and forth. "I'm sorry!" she told Meat. "I can't talk about it! I just can't talk about it!"

Meat and Herculeah were in Herculeah's living room. Herculeah was on the sofa, slumped forward. Her father had sent her home, saying, "I'll be over to get you when we're through here." "Through here," Herculeah knew, meant when the body was removed.

"Just tell me if it's Madame Rosa who's dead. I don't even know that much."

"Yes, it's Madame Rosa!"

"Well, you don't have to yell at me. I didn't do it."

Meat turned back to the window and watched the scene across the street. There were three police cars and an ambulance parked at the curb in front of Madame Rosa's. All the vehicles had their roof lights flashing, but there was no action that he could see, so he filled in the silence by saying, "I once consulted her."

Herculeah didn't answer, so he cleared his throat and said, "Did you hear what I said? I once consulted Madame Rosa."

This time he got Herculeah's attention. "You?"

He nodded.

"About what?"

"Something personal."

She waited.

Meat shrugged. "Well, I guess nobody ever consults a palmist about something impersonal."

"No," Herculeah agreed.

"I was going to tell you about it one time, but when I brought up Madame Rosa's name, you started making fun of people who go to have their palms read, and I stopped."

"I didn't make fun."

"Yes you did. You said that fortune-tellers don't really look at your hands, they watch your face for reactions. Like if the palmist says, 'I see a dark-haired man in your life,' and you frown, then the palmist quickly adds, 'but a fair-haired man will be the love of your life.' You acted it out. I remember it perfectly."

"Well, I didn't mean anything by it." Herculeah's gray eyes suddenly seemed to focus on Meat for the first time. "So why did you consult her?"

"About my dad."

"You wanted her to help find your dad?"

He nodded. "Well, actually, I just wanted any information I could get. I don't know where my dad is, what he does, anything. It's terrible not to know who your father is. He could be anybody—a criminal, that homeless guy that directs traffic, that mime who's all the time bothering me. I saw him today. I had to cross the street."

"Your dad is not the mime. The mime is closer to our age."

"He could be somebody just as bad."

"What did Madame Rosa tell you?"

"Well, first she said she needed something that had belonged to him. So I went home and I looked and looked. I didn't know what I was looking for until finally, way down in my mom's stocking drawer, I found one stocking with some things tied in the toe. Can you believe that my mom would hide things in the toe of a stocking?"

"Like what?"

"Jewelry and stuff, some old coins. The main item was a man's wedding ring, and inside was the date May 17, 1975, which is the day they got married.

"I went back to Madame Rosa and gave her the ring. She held the ring in her hands like this." Meat made a gesture as if he were washing his hands. He closed his eyes.

"She said, 'This is a wedding ring.' I thought, Well sure. That is real brilliant. I don't need a fortune-teller to tell me that, but I kept my mouth shut, which was not easy, because this was going to cost me ten dollars.

"Then she said, 'Your father wore this ring,' only she said, 'Yo fadda wore dis ring.' You know how she talks—talked."

Tears filled Herculeah's eyes, and she blotted them on the sleeve of her shirt.

"I better stop telling you this," Meat said. "I only brought it up to take your mind off the—off what happened, and now I've made you cry."

"No, I want you to go on. I'm interested."

"Oh, all right." Meat gave one quick glance out the window to make sure nothing was happening at Madame Rosa's before he continued. "Madame Rosa was still doing her hands like this"—more washing movements—"and then she got very still and said, 'I hear music.' I was thrilled. I suddenly got this great image of my father as Leonard Bernstein, hair falling all over everywhere, like a god, commanding music from everyday mortals."

Herculeah tried to smile.

"'A conductor,' I said. It wasn't a question. It was a fact. It was the realest thing I ever saw in my life. I was ready to run out and start going to concerts so I could find him."

"And you were right?"

Meat's animation drained away. "Of course not. Madame Rosa shook her head. 'No conductor.'

"I said, 'He played in an orchestra?' That was the next best thing I could think of. 'Violin?' I could live with that. Again she shook her head. Her eyes were closed, and then she opened them and looked at me so hard I thought she could see into my brain. She said, 'I see shoes.'"

"Shoes?" Herculeah asked.

"That's what I said. 'Shoes? My father sold shoes?' I thought of that awful old man in the shoe department at Belk's. But she shook her head again. And then she said the most surprising thing of all. 'Your fadda danced.'"

"Danced? Your father danced?"

"That's what she said."

"I can't imagine you with a father who danced."

Meat looked at her to see if this was an insult, but

Herculeah looked back with her clear gray eyes, and he was satisfied.

"To be honest, I can't either."

"What else did she say?"

"Nothing. That was all. Another customer came, and I had been a walk-in. I pulled out my ten dollars, but she wouldn't take it. She said, 'You come back. I work on this some more.'

"I went home. I was very upset. My mother was talking on the telephone. I said, 'Madame Rosa says my father was a dancer.' My mother slammed down the phone. I don't even know who she had been talking to. She looked up at me. Her eyes got very little. She stood up. She went out the door. I followed. I said, 'Where are you going?' She said, 'To tell that witch to mind her own business. I could kill that woman.'"

Meat broke off his narrative and pressed his face against the window. "Oh, the paramedics are getting the stretcher out of the ambulance. They're going up the steps. They're in the house. . . . Nothing's happening. . . . Oh, they're coming out. There's a body on the stretcher. They're sliding it in the ambulance. They're closing the doors. They're getting in."

There was a silence and then Meat said, "There's your dad. He's got on that jacket that doesn't match his pants and that tie that doesn't match anything. Now the ambulance is driving away."

He turned away from the window. "You know what I found out? You know how on TV they're always putting plastic bags on the victim's hands—to keep the clues in? Well, in real life, they use paper bags. Ask your dad if you don't believe me. So right now, Madame Rosa's hands—"

"My dad's probably coming to get me," Herculeah said abruptly, as if to shut him up. She got to her feet. "He wants me to go through the house."

"I'll go with you."

"No."

"I'll wait for you."

"Just go home."

"Your dad might want to ask me some questions. I might have seen something that would help. I did pass Madame Rosa's house on my way home today."

"You didn't even see me in the upstairs window, rapping on the glass."

Meat had turned back to the window and didn't answer. "Oh, your dad's going back in the house."

Herculeah walked quickly to the front door. Meat followed anxiously. "Didn't your dad tell you to wait here?"

"Yes."

Herculeah pulled on her sweater.

"Well, shouldn't you do what he says? He is in charge, you know."

"Not of me."

"Well, of the investigation. You should do what he says."

Herculeah swirled out the door. Her hair brushed Meat's arm as she passed.

"Well, wait for me," he said. "I'm coming, too."

6

SCENE OF THE CRIME

Herculeah drew near the crowd. She moved hesitantly, almost shyly, anxious to blend in with the onlookers.

She was afraid she might be recognized as the person who had discovered the body, and she did not want the attention that would bring. She glanced around. The people in the crowd were all strangers. She imagined that neighbors were watching from their windows.

Herculeah stopped beside a woman with a baby on her hip. The woman leaned around her baby and said to Herculeah, "They just brought the body out. You missed it. I couldn't see who it was, though."

Behind Herculeah a man's voice said, "Madame Rosa, I heard."

"She must have been murdered or there wouldn't be so many cops, don't you think? There's three carloads."

"Knifed, I heard."

"Maybe somebody didn't like their fortune."

There was nervous laughter from people who knew they shouldn't be laughing. Herculeah shivered. She had not felt warm since she had found Madame Rosa. The radios in the police cars droned on, though not even the policemen were paying attention.

A reporter was standing in front of the police barricade, getting ready to be filmed for a segment on the eleven o'clock news.

On cue, she said, "This is the home of Madame Rosa, fortune-teller, the scene today of a brutal crime."

Herculeah thought she could go up to the reporter and say, "I found the body. I looked all over the house for Madame Rosa, and then I went in the room where she tells fortunes and I saw her foot. Then I lifted the black tablecloth and saw her body. You would be surprised at how long you can look at a dead body before your mind catches on to the fact of death."

At her elbow, Meat spoke in a low voice. "You shouldn't be here."

She glanced around, startled. "Why?"

"I mean, you know, because your dad told you to wait."

"Oh, that. I thought you meant . . . something else," she finished uneasily.

Herculeah had thought that she shouldn't be here because she was placing herself in danger.

She glanced around quickly, suddenly aware of the individuals in the crowd. One of these people—that woman, the man in the dark hat, even the woman beside her with the baby—any one of them could have killed Madame Rosa. And whoever it might be knew that she had been in the house, too.

"Oh, there's your dad," Meat said. "Lieutenant Jones, we're over here!" he called.

Herculeah pressed forward through the crowd to join her father.

Meat tried to follow, but the crowd had drawn together and now blocked his way. He ended up standing alone, his hands at his sides. He watched as Herculeah and her dad went up the stairs together to Madame Rosa's.

Meat's eyes were sharply focused on Herculeah and her father. He felt a stab of envy—not just because Herculeah was always on the inside of things, and he never was, but also because she had such a satisfactory father.

He could hear Herculeah's father saying, "Herculeah, I understand you've been to Madame Rosa's often." Meat wanted to cry out, "I was there once, Lieutenant Jones. Madame Rosa was going to help me find my father," but he didn't.

The crowd began to murmur.

"Who is she?"

"Do you think she found the body?"

"Do you suppose she's some sort of relative?"

"She could be the murderer."

On the porch, Herculeah paused. She seemed to balk at going inside. Her father put his arm around her shoulders. "You want to sit down for a minute?"

Herculeah glanced at the crowd of curious onlookers and shook her head.

Meat pushed forward protectively. He knew he could make this easier for Herculeah, but once again the crowd wouldn't let him through. "Excuse me," he said, "excuse me!" but no one paid him any attention.

By the time he finally got around the side of the crowd, Madame Rosa's door had closed.

7

FINGERPRINTS

Inside Madame Rosa's house, Herculeah's father repeated his question. "You've been here often, Herculeah?"

"Not often, no. I used to feed the parrot while she was away."

"How many times did you do that—one, five, ten?"

"More like ten."

"And you came every day?"

"Yes. She would be gone two or three days at a time, and I would come every day—usually after school."

"So you did come fairly often."

"I guess."

"And how did you happen to come today? You were looking after the parrot?"

She shook her head. "I was looking out the window and I noticed the parrot was out on the porch and the front door was open, and I knew something was wrong. I didn't know it would be . . ." She trailed off. "I didn't know it would be death," she said in a hard voice, as if she was forcing herself to face what had happened.

She turned to her father, her face pale with concern. "I really liked her, Dad. I never wanted to take money for looking after Tarot, but she always had some trick to make me take the money. And she knew I didn't believe in fortune-telling, but she had a sense of humor about it—she'd read my palm and tell me something funny. I really liked her."

"Others didn't?"

"I didn't say that. Don't make me say things I don't mean. I just meant that I liked her. Period."

"Sorry about that. So when you came in the house today, what happened?"

"Well, when I came in, it had already happened. She was dead, but I didn't know that."

"Let's see. She died at—" He consulted a notebook. "She died between three and three-thirty. They were able to pinpoint the time of death, since they got here so soon afterward."

"It was probably three-thirty when I came in the house. I knew right away something was wrong. The parrot's stand was overturned, pictures were upset. And there was something else I couldn't put my finger on—something out of place—something that shouldn't have been there or something that wasn't there. I looked around for Madame Rosa—I even went up-stairs."

She paused and shuddered slightly as she remembered hearing the footstep.

"Go on."

"When I was upstairs, I heard someone below in the living room or hall. It had to be the murderer."

"Maybe," her father said. "Let's start down here. Show me what you did when you came in."

"All right, but stay with me, Dad. This has upset me more than I'm showing."

He put his arm around her shoulder. "I just want you to walk through what you did. I'm right beside you."

As if in a dream, Herculeah went into the living room. Madame Rosa's body had been removed from the parlor, but three policemen were still busy—putting objects in bags, dusting for fingerprints.

"What was the first thing you did when you came in the house?" her father said.

"I turned on the lamp." She pantomimed that, then

she went through the rest of her actions—picking up the parrot stand, going to the entrance to the parlor, looking inside.

"But I didn't see her—only her boot was showing. It was easy to miss that, and I didn't even notice that the chair was overturned. I didn't even smell the blood. I guess I'm not very observant."

"You're doing fine."

"Then I went back in the kitchen. There was a pot on the stove. I moved it over here." She pointed to the pot.

She paused to look around. "Oh, yeah. I looked out the back door. I don't know why I did that."

"Did you see anything?"

"No."

"Then what?"

"Then I went upstairs."

She went out into the hall and stopped at the foot of the stairs. "Do I have to go up there?"

"It would help."

Sighing, Herculeah went up the stairs.

"I opened every door and looked inside. I ended up at the window that overlooks the street. I saw Meat on his way home and tried to get his attention, but I couldn't. That was when I heard the footstep downstairs. I picked up a metal candlestick—to use as a weapon—came downstairs, saw that the front door was open and nobody was there."

"Where is the candlestick?"

"I left it downstairs."

They started down the wide stairs together and entered the living room.

"This is the candlestick?"

"Yes." She swallowed. This was the hard part. "Then I called Mom, but I just got the answering machine. I straightened some pictures. Then I went into the parlor to pick up the chair—I don't know what made me do that. And I found the b-body."

"What'd you touch?"

"Just her wrist. Her hand was stretched out, and I put my fingers like that—" She touched her own wrist. "But there wasn't any pulse. Then I called you."

"Good girl."

"Dad, I think the murderer was in the house most of that time."

"It's possible."

"And also—I'm just remembering this—when I looked in the parlor—this was when I first came in the house—that big book on her table was open. When I came downstairs later, it was closed. Somebody was in this house with me, Dad."

"It's possible."

"Maybe some of the neighbors saw the person leave."

"We're checking with them, but the place is so

overgrown that somebody could slip through the shrubbery and get to the alley without being seen, particularly if it was someone familiar with the neighborhood."

Herculeah's shoulders sagged. "Can I go home now? I don't feel so good."

"In a minute. Frank wants to get your prints."

She drew back. "My fingerprints?"

"Yes."

"Dad, you don't think I did this?"

"Nobody thinks that, Herculeah. It's just that your fingerprints are all over the house and we need to eliminate them."

She looked down at her hands. Tears filled her eyes. "I did not do it!" she said.

8

THE MIME

Someone tapped Meat on the shoulder, and Meat screamed.

Meat had left the crowd and crossed the street—he did not want to be trapped behind them again. He now stood by Herculeah's walkway, waiting for Herculeah and her father to come out of Madame Rosa's. He was so intent that the touch actually terrified him.

He turned. He almost screamed again. It was the local mime, who had tapped him on the shoulder with his white-gloved hand.

Meat had never seen the mime up close before, because he always crossed the street whenever he saw him approaching. Meat would walk ten blocks out of his way to avoid contact with the painted white face now at his shoulder.

Beneath the white paint, the mime's features looked small and foreign. His eyes were unreadable.

"What do you want?" Meat asked, in a voice that was not quite steady.

The mime pointed to the police cars and asked in a series of exaggerated shrugs what had happened. Meat wanted to yell, "Speak English."

He did not. Also, Meat decided, he would not lower himself to pantomiming back. He said, "I believe Madame Rosa has been murdered."

There was another of those annoying, questioning poses from the mime.

"No one knows who did it," Meat said, speaking loudly, as if to someone hard of both hearing and understanding.

The mime now went into the various possibilities. He clutched his hands to his throat, strangling himself. He shot an imaginary pistol at himself and gripped his stomach in pain. He drank poison and rolled his eyes up in his head. He stabbed himself in the chest.

Meat nodded quickly and stabbed his own chest. He gave a shiver of disgust at himself for falling into the mime's trap.

He had seen it happen often in the park. A perfectly

normal person would be tricked into an imaginary tug-of-war with an invisible rope, or pulling a piece of invisible string out of the mime's mouth, or putting an imaginary coin in the mime's back.

Meat noticed that Herculeah and her dad were out on the porch now. He felt a wave of relief. "I'm sorry," he said, turning to the mime. "You'll have to excuse me now. . . ." But the mime was gone.

Meat recalled that no one ever saw the mime coming or going. He was just suddenly there, on a street corner or touching your shoulder. Meat gave a slight shudder, remembering the tap of that gloved hand.

Meat watched Herculeah and her dad intently as they crossed the street. Herculeah's father's arm was around her shoulders, and she looked dazed and miserable.

Meat's eyes burned with the desire to be part of their conversation, no matter how painful it was. As they came closer, Meat picked up the first scrap of conversation.

Herculeah's father was saying, "I'll stay with you till your mom gets home. Where is she anyway? Is she always this late?"

"I don't know. She told me where she was going, but I can't remember."

At that, Meat stepped forward purposefully. "I can answer that, Lieutenant Jones. Mrs. Jones is trying to find a missing dog."

Herculeah turned toward Meat as he spoke, but her look was blank, as if she couldn't place who he was. Her father's look was not one of gratitude, as Meat had hoped. Indeed, the lieutenant gave a snort of disgust.

"Wouldn't you know it," he said.

One of the reasons Herculeah's parents had divorced was because her father scorned her mother's detective work. Herculeah was too drained of emotion to be concerned about her father's antagonism now.

"Actually, it's more than a missing dog. It's a kidnapping. The dog has been kidnapped." Meat spoke very seriously, as if he were giving testimony. "The couple's getting a divorce, and the man kidnapped Trip—that's the dog—he was named for their vacation to Laguna Beach—and Mrs. Jones was hired by the wife to—"

Lieutenant Jones cut Meat off with a gesture that was so effective, Meat thought he must have perfected it in his police work.

Only Herculeah's look of distress gave Meat the courage to continue.

"I'll be glad to stay with Herculeah, sir, if you have to get back to"—he nodded in the direction of Madame Rosa's house—"you know, the scene of the crime."

"I've got time."

"So have I. I'm free till supper, and we're probably having leftovers, so—"

"Thanks anyway."

Suddenly Herculeah turned around and looked directly into Meat's eyes. Her eyes were filled with tears that began to spill over onto her pale cheeks. The misery in her face was so intense that Meat stepped back, almost falling off the curb.

"Meat," she said. "I had to be fingerprinted!"

Then she turned and ran into the house.

Meat stood without moving. Lieutenant Jones didn't seem to be able to move either.

"Herculeah couldn't kill anyone!" Meat burst out. "She's the most gentle person I know. She cares about everybody. She's strong but—"

"I know Herculeah couldn't kill anyone," Chico Jones interrupted angrily.

Meat's mother came around the corner then, a small bag of groceries in one arm. She stopped as she saw Meat and Lieutenant Jones together. Her eyes moved to the police cars in front of Madame Rosa's house.

"What happened?" she asked.

Meat looked at his mother. His eyes narrowed. He remembered that the only thing she had ever said about his father was "Good riddance." He remembered that when Madame Rosa had tried to help him—when she *had* helped him—at least told him his father had something to do with dance—his mother had put an end to any further help by going over to Madame Rosa's in a rage.

He remembered he had said, "Where are you going?"

He remembered she had answered, "To tell that witch to mind her own business. I could kill that woman."

"What has happened?" she asked again, with what Meat thought was false concern.

Meat spoke in a cold precise way. He was glad Lieutenant Jones was there to hear his words.

"You will be happy to know," he said, "that Madame Rosa has been murdered."

9

A SUSPECT

In the living room below, Herculeah's mother's voice rose with concern. "Chico, Herculeah thinks you suspect her!"

"I don't suspect her! That's ridiculous."

"Well, she thinks you do. She's in tears up there in her room."

"She's in tears because she found a murder victim. She needs to cry. She's not as hard and cold as you are, thank God."

Herculeah lay on her bed listening to her parents' angry voices below. Her mother had come home a half hour earlier, put Herculeah to bed, and then gone downstairs to talk to Chico. Herculeah wanted to get up and close the door, but she was exhausted.

"You didn't have to fingerprint her. She washed her hands five times before she got into bed."

"Look, Mim, our daughter was all over the house, she touched everything, and they just wanted her prints for purposes of elimination."

"It makes people feel guilty to be fingerprinted."

"Well, if you'd been home instead of out looking for a kidnapped dog—"

"Let's not get started on my jobs," Herculeah's mother said, cutting him off. There was a silence. Then in a more conversational tone she said, "As a matter of fact, I was never thrilled about her going to Madame Rosa's when nobody was there but that fool parrot."

"Then why didn't you stop her?"

"Have you ever tried to stop Herculeah from doing something she wanted to do? For some reason, Herculeah liked the woman."

"I take it there were people who didn't."

"That's right."

"Who? Any names?"

"No. She came to see me one time. Did I ever mention it to you?"

"No. When was this?"

"About a month ago."

Herculeah listened more intently now. She hadn't known Madame Rosa had consulted her mother.

"About what?"

"Well, she was vague. Apparently some woman had come to her for a consultation—she wouldn't tell me the woman's name. The woman wanted to know if Madame Rosa could tell whether someone was capable of murder."

"If she could do that, the department could have used her," Chico Jones said.

Mim continued thoughtfully, remembering. "I believe the woman's son had threatened her with a knife, and the woman was frightened."

"She could have come to us."

"She didn't think so. Anyway, Madame Rosa told the woman to bring her something belonging to the son. The woman came back with the knife itself."

"Did she describe the knife?"

"No. Madame Rosa took the knife in her hand and closed her eyes. After a moment, she became very upset. She dropped the knife as if she'd been burned and cried, 'Yes! Yes! Your boy will kill with this knife. Your boy will kill!' Then she was so overcome that she fainted. When she came to, the woman and the knife were gone."

"And she never gave you a name?"

"No, but I got the feeling it was someone local, because Madame Rosa was afraid for her own life. She was afraid the son might find out what his mother had done and come after her. She began to ramble then, talking about the month not being auspicious—cards, bad omens, things like that. Finally I broke in and asked, what was it exactly that she wanted me to do. She said, 'That is the trouble. There is nothing anyone can do.'"

Listening upstairs, Herculeah thought her mother did a good job of imitating Madame Rosa's voice. But then Madame Rosa had a distinctive voice.

"I told her she should go to the police. She said, 'But I have no proof. I only have'—she put her hand on her chest—'a feeling.' Even though I don't believe in that sort of thing, Chico, the way she said the word 'feeling' made me shiver."

"Anything more?"

"No, she got up then and left. I really didn't take the thing seriously, although maybe I should have. After all, she was killed with a knife."

"Yes."

"But do you think the two things could be connected?"

"It's possible."

The phone rang then, interrupting the conversation. Her mother answered, "Mim Jones."

She listened and said, "Yes, he's right here. It's for you, Chico."

Her father's voice made a series of nothing remarks—"Yes. . . . No. . . . None? . . . I see. . . . Yes, it does look that way."

He hung up the phone. Herculeah raised up on one elbow to hear what her father was going to say.

He said, "They just got the results of the fingerprints."

Herculeah got to her feet and moved toward the door. Her hand covered her heart.

"The only fingerprints on the knife were Madame Rosa's."

Herculeah didn't wait to hear any more. "She didn't kill herself!" she yelled.

She ran out into the hall.

"She didn't! There was somebody downstairs. I don't care what you say—Madame Rosa didn't kill herself!"

She flew down the stairs. Her parents came into the hallway and looked up at her. Their faces were lined in mutual concern.

"Go back to bed," her mother said. "I'm coming up to talk to you." She turned to Herculeah's father. "You'd better go, Chico. She's had too much for one day."

"I agree," her father said. "I want to say one thing first."

"You've already said too much."

"Herculeah, I'm very sorry you got drawn into this—sorrier than you can imagine. However, I never once thought that your involvement was anything other than the very unfortunate accident of finding the body."

"Are you through, Chico? Will you please go now?"

"No, I am not through." He looked up at Herculeah. "Hon, you did everything exactly right. You didn't touch anything vital. You called the police. You gave us your help.

"But now, your involvement is over. I will keep you posted on anything you need to know. In the meantime, I want you to get on with your life and leave this investigation to us."

Herculeah paused. The strength that had sent her flying down the stairs now left her. She put out one hand and gripped the banister for support.

"She did not kill herself," she said stubbornly.

"On that point we agree," her father said.

10

A Key at Midnight

Herculeah awoke at midnight. She was so twisted in her covers that she had to work to free herself. She got to her feet. She saw her moonlit reflection in the mirror.

The ribbon that had bound her hair had come loose, and her hair was extra wild. She smoothed it down and went into the hall.

The house was quiet. Slowly, she started down the steps.

Her first thought when she awoke was not of Madame Rosa. She had not even dreamed of Madame

Rosa, as she had feared she might. Her thoughts were of Tarot. What had become of the parrot? Who had taken him? She should have thought to do that herself.

In the morning she would call her dad and find out. He might let her keep him until a relative was found. She recalled there was only one.

Herculeah walked into the darkened living room. She crossed to the window where she had stood just that afternoon. It seemed a long time ago.

She looked up the street at Madame Rosa's house. Then she rested her forehead against the cool glass.

Outside, the street was deserted. There had been a light rain, and the streetlights gave a soft glow to the parked cars. She lifted her head and glanced again at Madame Rosa's house. Her look sharpened.

There was a light on in the living room downstairs. She could see a thin crack of light through the partly opened draperies. Herculeah didn't think the strip of light had been there when she first looked. If it had not been, then someone had just turned on the light.

She tried to shake off the thought. I do have too much imagination, she thought with a sigh.

She glanced down, saw the binoculars, and picked them up. She lifted them to her face. She noticed two things.

1. The police barricade had been broken.
2. The light was no longer there.

From the doorway her mother said, "Herculeah, what are you doing at the window?"

"Mom, listen, I woke up and I thought about Tarot and I came downstairs. I was just standing here at the window, and I noticed that a light was on in Madame Rosa's living room. And then I picked up the binocs to check it out and the light went away. Either someone turned off the light or someone pulled the drapes closed. Mom, somebody's over there. If you don't believe me, look, the police barricade's down."

"Anybody could have broken that. Anyway, this is your father's business. You can call him in the morning."

"But, Mom, in the morning he'll be gone. And what if it's the murderer?"

"If it's the murderer, it's up to your father to catch him, not us. You heard what your father said. He wants you to stay out of this, and for once I agree with him. Now, good night."

"Mom, just let me tell you one thing."

"I'm listening."

"We could go over there. We could check it out. Mom, listen, I've got the key."

"What key?"

"The key to Madame Rosa's. She gave it to me so I could look after the parrot."

"Where is this key?"

"In my drawer upstairs. I'll go get it."

"We'll both go get it."

"Mom, you'll actually do this?" Herculeah asked. She didn't feel tired at all now. She was always exhilarated by investigation. "We're going?"

"We are going to bed, young lady."

"Mom, you know I hate it when you call me 'young lady.'"

"In this case, it's a compliment. I could call you a lot of other things."

"Like what?"

"If you are trying to distract me from that key, you have not succeeded. I want it." She held out her hand. "And I want it now."

"Oh, all right."

Her mother took Herculeah by the arm and led her upstairs. She waited at the door to Herculeah's room.

Herculeah went into her room, opened her top drawer, and took the key out of the old cigar box where she kept her valuables.

She handed it to her mother. "There."

"Thank you," her mother said.

Herculeah watched as her mother went into her

bedroom. She listened as her mother opened a drawer and dropped the key inside.

Herculeah knew which drawer her mother had opened—the one in her bedside table. Satisfied, Herculeah went back to bed.

11

THE SHADOW

"Do you get the feeling we're being followed?" Herculeah asked uneasily.

"Who would follow us?"

"I don't know," Herculeah said. "The Shadow," she added in a theatrical voice. She glanced over her shoulder. "I don't know. Meat, I have the feeling that I saw something yesterday afternoon that ought to make sense to me and it doesn't. Or maybe somebody thinks I saw something. It's like I'm in a daze."

"I know. That's why we've come to the flea market—to take your mind off it."

"There was something wrong about that body."

"Yes, it was dead."

Herculeah grimaced.

"You want my opinion, Herculeah?"

"About what?"

"About why she was killed?"

Herculeah glanced at him.

"Blackmail," he finished.

"Why blackmail?" Herculeah asked.

"Because people told her things, like I spilled my guts about my dad. Herculeah, you get in that little room, and it's like being in a psychiatrist's office—only darker and more secret. You tell things."

"Maybe."

"Take it from me. You tell things."

Meat and Herculeah were making their way through the open-air part of the flea market. They sidestepped around baby strollers, young kids with Sno-Kones and cotton candy, families of shoppers.

"I saw Madame Rosa in here once," Meat said. "She was handing out flyers. I took one."

"Do you remember what it said?"

"'I know your future—do you?' That was in big letters. Below that, it said she did readings, contacted departed loved ones, located missing people—that was what made me go to her about my dad. But, of course, she didn't help me—at least she didn't get to finish helping me."

The flea market was spread over the grounds of an old cotton warehouse. During the week, it was nothing but a stretch of cracked tarmac and a dusty field, but on the weekends, the vendors set up booths or sold from the backs of station wagons or from blankets on the ground. There were music and balloons in the air.

In the old warehouse itself were permanent booths—concession stands, furniture and antique stalls, a puppet show, and a video-game arcade.

Herculeah looked at Meat. "You're uneasy, too."

"I am not."

"I can always tell."

"How?"

"You go like this." Herculeah narrowed her eyes and glanced suspiciously from side to side.

"I do not."

Herculeah smiled. "You know what I'm going to do? I'm going to buy myself a good-luck charm."

"An amulet," Meat suggested. "I get that in crossword puzzles sometimes. That's what you want. It means an old charm."

"Good-luck charms have to be old. They have to have worked at one time or another."

"I think amulets hang around your neck."

"Then that's exactly what I want."

"Everything's half-price," a woman in a straw hat

told them, stretching her arms out over a table of socks and underwear.

Herculeah shook her head. "We're looking for something special."

She paused to check out an assortment of beads and bracelets spread out on a blanket. "You see anything you like?" the lady asked.

"I'm looking for something old. An amulet."

"An amu-what?" the lady said.

"Never mind."

"The real old stuff's inside the warehouse," Meat said.

They went through the wide doors and were immediately approached by a man in Levi's.

"Help you?" he asked.

"I'm looking for old jewelry."

"I got earrings, nose rings, hand rings, toe rings, bracelets, necklaces, anklets—you name it, I got it."

"Where are the necklaces?"

"Right back here."

The necklaces were hanging from an old towel rack, and Herculeah looked through them slowly. "Would you call that an amulet?" she asked Meat, showing him a crystal attached to a chain.

"No—well, maybe. I don't know. I never actually saw one of the things before."

She closed her hand around it. "I don't get a feeling that it's lucky."

Again, she let her hands roam over the necklaces. She closed her eyes, then said, "Now that feels lucky. What do you think, Meat?"

She showed him a chain with an acorn-shaped pendant suspended from it.

"Well, it looks old, anyway."

Herculeah turned to the man. "Can I try this silver one on?"

He unlocked the rack and Herculeah slipped the necklace over her head. "I wonder if there's anything inside," she asked, fingering the necklace. "It looks like the top comes off. Does it?"

"It's probably something real valuable in there, missy."

"I bet," Herculeah said.

"I didn't want to pry the top off," the vendor explained. "It's too valuable a piece to ruin."

"How valuable?"

"I'd have to have five dollars for that—'cause you're not just getting a chain and a silver antique acorn thing. You're also getting whatever's inside."

"I'll give you three."

"Three dollars! Missy, the chain alone's worth three dollars." He gave her a pained expression. "Four," he said.

"Three-fifty."

More pain. He shook his head. "Missy, you drive a hard bargain. It's a deal."

Herculeah smiled—her first real smile of the day. She turned to Meat. "Lend me three-fifty," she said.

"You don't have any money?"

"Not with me."

Meat sighed and pulled out some money. "If there's anything valuable in there, I get half of it," he said.

"I promise, but it doesn't want to open—I tried to force it when the man wasn't looking."

"You better leave it alone. The good luck might get out," Meat said.

They walked away with Herculeah smiling down at her amulet. She glanced at Meat.

"I want a Sno-Kone. Do you?"

"I don't suppose you have any money for those either."

"No."

He sighed. "Oh, come on."

They walked to the Sno-Kone stand, and a woman in a baseball cap said, "What flavor?"

"Rainbow," said Herculeah.

"Same," said Meat.

They took their cones and began walking again. Herculeah's cone had already begun to drip, but she didn't care. She felt good.

"It's amazing what a Sno-Kone and an amulet can do for you," she said, grinning at Meat. "Maybe you ought to get one."

They started back down the aisle. As they passed the booth where Herculeah had bought the amulet, Meat paused. "I want to ask this guy something."

"I'll be over here," Herculeah answered, nodding to a booth that sold used books.

Meat approached the man. "Can I ask you a question?"

"Sure."

"There used to be a woman, a fortune-teller, who handed out flyers here."

"Yeah, Madame Rosa. She had a booth down across from the puppet theater. She stopped coming here, though."

"Do you know why?"

The man shook his head. "She came flying out of here a few Saturdays ago like the devil himself was after her. I stopped her. I said, 'Lady, you need some help?' The woman was as white as if she'd seen a ghost. She muttered something about a knife. I said, 'Somebody pulled a knife on you? You want me to call security?'

"She looked at me. I'll never forget that look as long as I live. I asked again, 'Did somebody pull a knife on you?' And she answered—and I'll never forget this, either—'No, but they will.'"

12

KILLER PUPPETS

"Puppets!" Herculeah lifted her head. She said, "I hear puppets."

Over the loudspeaker an artificially high voice was chirping, "It's time for us to go on."

"It is not. It's five minutes before we go on."

"Frankie said it's time for us to go on riiiight now."

"What does Frankie know?"

"Frankie knows more than we do."

"Huh! He wouldn't be anything without us."

"Well, we wouldn't be much without him."

"Huh."

"Well, anyway, it's time for us to go on."

"It is not—hey, you're right. It is time for us to go on. Everybody on stage. It's time for us to go on."

Herculeah said, "Come on. I feel like watching puppets."

"I hate puppets," Meat said.

"You can't hate puppets, Meat. They're toys."

"I hate puppets. I hate mimes. I hate clowns. I have a real reason for hating puppets, though," he said as he reluctantly followed Herculeah toward the show.

"What's that?"

"There was this girl in my kindergarten class and she wore mittens that were like puppets. One was a dog and one was a cat. And she'd come up to me and say in a high voice, 'You better pet us or we'll bite you,' and I'd reach out to pet the stupid things and before I could, they'd bite me. And it hurt. And she only did it to me. She'd let everybody else pet them. I was the only one they bit."

"Oh, Meat, mittens can't hurt."

"These could. They had teeth—little pearls. Killer puppets, I called them."

Meat broke off his story to say, "I bet that's Madame Rosa's booth over there. The amulet guy said it was across from the theater."

Herculeah turned and looked at the empty booth. She could imagine Madame Rosa there, laying out her cards, bending over palms. Unbidden, tears filled her eyes and she curled her fingers around her amulet.

"He told me something else. Madame Rosa saw something that terrified her. She saw it somewhere here in the flea market. And that's not all. She was muttering something about a—"

"Tell me later, Meat. We need to back up and let these little kids up front," Herculeah said.

The children arranged themselves on the floor in front of the curtain. The curtain opened and Frankie, the puppeteer, stuck his head out.

"She was muttering something about a knife," Meat whispered.

Herculeah looked at him then, but her question was drowned out by the puppeteer's hearty, "Hi, gang!"

"Hi."

"Let's try that again. I didn't hear you. Hi!"

"HI!"

"That's better."

Herculeah wanted to ask about the knife, but her eyes focused on the puppeteer.

"Who is he?" she asked Meat in a whisper.

"Some guy."

"He looks familiar."

The puppeteer said, "Want to get on with the show?"

"Yes."

"I didn't hear you."

"YES!"

The head of the first puppet appeared. It was a prince.

"There's something familiar about him, too," Herculeah mumbled.

"I read somewhere that the puppeteer models his characters on real people," Meat whispered back.

The prince looked up at the sky. "Ah, beautiful night! Bring forth my loved one!" Then to the crowd he said, "I am waiting here for the most beautiful girl in the world."

The ogre's head appeared behind him, bringing cries of delight from the audience.

The prince swirled around, but the ogre was gone. "Did you see her?" he asked the audience.

"YES!"

"Was she not the most beautiful girl in the world?"

"NO!"

"I will try again. O beautiful night, bring forth my loved one."

A witch appeared, flying down from above and disappearing almost immediately on the other side of the stage.

The audience laughed in delight. Again the prince asked, "Oh, did you see her?"

"YES!"

"Was she not beautiful?"

"NO!"

Herculeah reached for Meat's hand and held it. Meat was so stunned that for a moment he almost made a terrible mistake and jerked his hand away.

He glanced at Herculeah, but her eyes were on the stage.

"Did you see the witch?" she asked.

"Yes."

"Did you notice anything about her?"

"Not really."

"Not even who she looked like?"

"No."

"Madame Rosa."

13

WHICH WITCH

The show had ended. The puppeteer had taken up a collection, and he had reminded the audience, "There'll be another show at four o'clock—a completely different show. Don't miss it. This one's going to be sca-a-a-ry!"

Herculeah and Meat followed him backstage.

"Hi, I'm Herculeah Jones," she said. "We really enjoyed your show."

"Well, thanks. I'm hoping for a bigger audience at four. Come back. Check it out."

"I think it's really neat the way you model your puppets on real people."

The puppeteer's look sharpened. "I've seen you around somewhere. Let me think."

"Her mom's a private eye," Meat said, more to get into the conversation than to be helpful.

The puppeteer turned his sharp gaze on Meat. "I've seen her sign, over on . . ."

He paused as if waiting for Meat to supply the name of the street, but Herculeah interrupted.

"Are all of your puppets based on real people? I thought I recognized one."

"Hey, maybe I'll do a puppet of you sometime," the puppeteer said, sidestepping the question. "You'd make a good . . . let me see . . . Amazon."

Meat looked quickly at Herculeah to see if she had been insulted, but she was smiling, apparently pleased.

"You'd have to use a lot of yarn for my hair," Herculeah said.

"Well, don't do one of me," Meat interrupted, "or you'd have to use a lot of—" He stopped abruptly.

"Stuffing," the puppeteer finished.

Meat turned away as if he'd been slapped. He did feel insulted. He wasn't secure like Herculeah.

"Can I ask you something else?" Herculeah said.

"Shoot."

"You used to know Madame Rosa, didn't you?"

"Who?"

"Madame Rosa. She had that booth over there."
Herculeah pointed to the now-empty booth across the
way.

"Oh, her."

"Herculeah was the person who found her body,"
Meat said. At least when he did get into the conversation, he had something interesting to say.

The puppet in Frank's hands took an involuntary
step in midair.

"Yeah, well, she had that booth, but she hasn't been
here in a while. I can't even remember the last time I
saw her."

"Did you ever notice who her customers were?"

"Mostly women."

"Any regulars?"

"I didn't watch that closely. It looked like an impulse
thing. People would see her sign and, 'Hey, I think I'll
find out about old Uncle Abe's will.'"

Herculeah smiled, but Meat didn't. A sudden
thought hit him. "I was just talking to that guy who
sells jewelry, and he said that Madame Rosa came running out of here like she'd seen a ghost—like the devil
himself was after her—that's the way he put it."

The puppeteer gave a shrug. "So?"

"So I was wondering if you saw anything that could
have scared her."

"No, but I was probably in the middle of a show. I

don't notice anything then but the puppets. Man, I've got a cast of hundreds."

Herculeah was watching him intently. "I noticed the witch sort of resembled Madame Rosa. Was that on purpose?"

"Nah, I've had that puppet for years."

"Her cloak was like the witch's too."

"A cloak's a cloak—a piece of black cloth. Look, it's been nice talking with you, but I got another show in fifteen minutes."

"Thanks for your time," Herculeah said.

Herculeah and Meat walked away from the theater, past the stalls and booths, and out into the open air. They started for home.

"That man," Herculeah said, "knows something he's not telling."

"You might as well finish your statement," Meat said tiredly.

Herculeah looked at him, puzzled.

"'That man knows something he's not telling . . .'" Meat repeated, then he supplied the ending, "'and I'm going to find out what.'"

Herculeah smiled grimly.

14

FOGGING OUT

Herculeah and Meat were sitting across from each other in Herculeah's kitchen. They both stared down at the papers in front of them on the table.

"You make up a list of suspects," Herculeah had said to Meat, "and I will, too. Then we'll compare notes."

Herculeah was eating a toasted peanut butter and carrot sandwich as she worked on her list.

So far she had:

1. Madame Rosa's last remaining relative.
2. Someone Madame Rosa was blackmailing.

3. The boy whose mother had consulted Madame Rosa about the knife.
4. Meat's mother.

Herculeah realized she couldn't show the list to Meat, because his mother was on it. She glanced at him across the table. He was nervously tapping the point of his pencil on the table.

So far, Meat had three items on his list:

1. The mime.

He had been so ashamed after he wrote this that he was going to erase it, but Herculeah had given him a pencil without an eraser. Also there had been something about the mime's unreadable eyes that still troubled him.

He added:

2. The puppeteer.
3. Any clowns in the area.

Now he was even more ashamed of his list. However, he had always had a deep suspicion of anyone hiding in a clown suit.

"You're sure you don't want one of these?" Herculeah asked, indicating her sandwich. "This is the first time I've been able to eat anything since the—since yesterday." She still liked to avoid the word *murder*.

"No, thanks," he lied.

She put down her sandwich and crossed out Meat's mother's name.

"Who are you crossing out?" he asked, looking at her sharply.

"Nobody important." She smiled. "That's why I'm crossing them out. You know who my best suspect is? I don't know if I told you this, but Madame Rosa came to talk to my mom."

"Oh? Why didn't she just look in the future?"

"Meat, be serious. This could be important. Some woman came to Madame Rosa because her son had threatened her. She wanted Madame Rosa to tell her if the threat was real or not. Madame Rosa told her the same thing she told you about your dad. 'You gotta bring me something belonging to the boy.' Now I'm imitating her."

"What'd she bring?"

"She brought the knife."

"The same knife she was stabbed with?"

"We don't know that. Anyway, Madame Rosa took the knife—like she did your father's ring—only the vibes were so terrible, so threatening that she fainted. When she came to, the woman and the knife were gone." She smiled ruefully. "But I think the woman had her answer."

"Who was the woman?"

"Madame Rosa didn't say."

Meat was staring intently at Herculeah's sandwich. She noticed and said, "I'll put pickles on it."

"On what?"

"The sandwich."

"No, I better not. Even if I do get to be six feet four, it wouldn't take all that many peanut butter sandwiches to fill me out."

"Dill pickles."

"Oh, all right, I'll have a peanut butter and pickle sandwich, but hold the carrots. Then he added, "Open face." He felt easier after this decision.

Herculeah put the sandwich on a paper towel and set it before Meat. Then she said, "Maybe I ought to try putting on my glasses."

"What?"

"Those glasses that make me think better."

"How would that help?"

"I don't know. There are a lot of things I don't understand. Anyway, it can't hurt. I need to fog out."

Herculeah went into the living room and came back with her pair of granny glasses. She had bought these in a secondhand store on Antique Row because when she put them on they turned the world into a blur and allowed her to think better.

She unfolded the glasses and looked at them. "The trouble is that as far as I'm concerned, the whole world is already a blur."

She hooked the thin metal hoops around her ears and stared into the thick glass.

Meat waited in silence as long as he could. "Nothing?" he asked finally.

"Well, I wouldn't call it nothing."

"What?"

"I see that room."

"The scene of the crime?"

"I see those pictures . . ."

"What pictures?"

"Madame Rosa had family pictures lined up on this old chest. They were relatives—a dozen of them, she told me once. She also told me that they were all dead but one. Then she said two, because she forgot to count herself."

Meat bent forward over his sandwich.

"There was a picture of Madame Rosa with a child— a boy," Herculeah was saying thoughtfully, "but I didn't see it that afternoon—not when I came back downstairs. I wonder if the murderer took it."

"She could have gotten rid of it herself."

"I don't think so. Those pictures were always there— only that afternoon they had been disturbed. And when I was straightening them—waiting for my mom to answer the phone—I couldn't find that picture."

"Maybe you overlooked it."

Herculeah took off her glasses and looked directly

into Meat's eyes. "I want to go back in that house and see if that picture is there."

"You can't."

"Why not?"

"You can't break in. Didn't you learn anything from breaking into Dead Oaks last month?"

"Yes, I learned that it's a lot easier when you have a key."

"So where are you going to get a key?"

"From my mother's drawer upstairs."

Meat stared at her with his mouth slightly open.

"But, of course," she said, "we'll have to wait till dark."

Meat sighed. "Of course." He took the last bite of his sandwich.

"Beware! Beware!" a raucous voice screamed from upstairs.

Meat put his hand over his chest where his sandwich had lodged in a hard, painful knot. "What was that?" he gasped.

"Just Tarot," Herculeah said. "Didn't I tell you? My dad agreed I could keep him until they find Madame Rosa's relative."

"You could have warned me."

Herculeah grinned. "Beware, beware."

"Thanks a lot."

15

WALK-INS UNWELCOME

"Your father would definitely not approve of this," Meat said sternly.

It was night. Herculeah and Meat were slowly walking up the sidewalk to Madame Rosa's house.

Herculeah didn't answer. In her pocket, her fingers curled around the key to the front door. In her other hand was a flashlight.

"And my mother wouldn't approve, either," Meat added. He was talking out of nervousness. "Though half the reason I'm doing this is because I'm mad at my mom."

Herculeah paused at the walkway. The sign was still

there. Herculeah clicked on the flashlight and shone it on the sign. "See, Meat, it says 'Walk-ins Welcome.'"

"That makes me feel so much better," Meat said.

Herculeah glanced up and down the street. No cars or people were in sight.

"Quick," she said, "before somebody comes."

She opened the gate and pulled Meat in behind her. Meat was always amazed at Herculeah's strength. Then almost before he knew what was happening, she had closed the gate and the two of them were pressed against the thick shrubbery.

"A car's coming!"

Herculeah slipped into the shrubbery as easily as if she were a cat. Meat, trying to follow, crashed forward like a hippo.

The car went by slowly. "That looked like a cop car," Herculeah said.

"I wouldn't know," Meat said. He was still facedown in the shrubbery. "Could it have been your dad?"

"No, he doesn't drive a black-and-white. I think that's the same police car that's been driving by every hour. I told my dad about seeing the light in the house last night. That's probably why they're still checking. Anyway, the car's gone now."

Meat started backing out of the bushes, but Herculeah held him. "Sometimes they go around the block and come right back."

"Oh." Meat settled in for a wait. "So who were the people on your list of suspects? You never told me."

"Nobody important. You?"

"Same."

"Though I did put down that it could be Madame Rosa's last living relative, but I just did that because my dad says most murders are committed by someone the victim knows."

She broke off as car lights passed, lighting up the fence. "See, aren't you glad we're not up on the porch unlocking the door?" she whispered.

"Yes," Meat said firmly. That was, it seemed to him, the only thing he had to be glad about in this terrible evening.

When the police car disappeared for the second time, Herculeah said the words Meat had been dreading, "Let's go inside."

They climbed out of the shrubbery. Keeping to the shadows, they moved up the steps.

"You wait there out of sight"—she indicated a chair—"while I unlock the door. The lock's old. Sometimes I have to work to get the door open."

Meat stood behind the chair. "Remember the last time you broke into a house?"

"This isn't breaking—I have the key."

"I wonder if there's anything in there about my dad. Did she keep files?"

"I never saw any."

"I sure would like to see the file on my dad, if there is one." He watched Herculeah's efforts with the key. "Maybe somebody else might want the same thing— their file. That could be the reason somebody's return-ing to the house."

"You could be right, Meat. You really could."

Meat felt a moment of pleasure, heightened by the fact that the lock wasn't turning.

"There's something I've been meaning to ask you. What does your mom do when she wants to find a missing person?"

"Well, right now, she's looking for a missing dog—" She broke off, turned abruptly, and faced him. "You know what you could do? I read about this in 'Dear Abby'. When you want to locate a missing parent— you can't do it for a missing boyfriend or something like that, it has to be a parent or a child. Anyway, you write to—I think it's the Salvation Army, give them the information, and they help you." She turned the key again.

"But that's wonderful news. You should have told me sooner."

"Ah, more good news."

"What?"

"The door's open. We can go inside now."

16

FOOTSTEPS

"I'm going to make sure the curtains are closed all the way, because the other night I saw a sliver of light in the window—at least I think I did," Herculeah said. "I wouldn't want that to happen to us."

Herculeah crossed the living room and gave the draperies a tug. "There," she said.

From the doorway Meat said weakly, "I could never be a burglar."

"What brought that on?"

"Being in strange houses makes me feel faint."

"Well, this will only take a minute. Sit out in the

hall, why don't you? There's a straight-backed chair right by the door."

"I probably should sit down. Then if I do faint, I won't have far to fall."

Meat sank down into the chair. Moonlight came in through the hall windows, and Meat could see Madame Rosa's cloak hanging on the coatrack.

"Hurry up," he said in the empty hallway.

"Anyway, we're not burglars. We're not stealing anything."

As Herculeah spoke, she moved to the old buffet and clicked on the flashlight. She shone the beam over the dusty surface, then on the pictures, one by one.

"The picture of Madame Rosa and the boy isn't here," she called triumphantly. "I knew it wouldn't be."

"Why does that make you happy?"

"Because it proves my suspicion that there's something important about that missing picture—some connection with Madame Rosa's murder. That boy in the photograph was probably her last remaining relative, though he would be a man by now."

"So, can we go?" Meat asked from the hallway, glancing uneasily at the empty cloak.

"I just want to check one more thing."

Meat thought she sounded like his dentist. He slumped forward in misery.

"So what is this one thing?" he asked. "I bet it's going to be one thing, then one more thing. We'll probably be here till dawn." His voice cracked with despair.

"I want to have a look at that book on Madame Rosa's table."

Herculeah's voice grew fainter as she moved into the parlor. "The book was open when I first got here, and then somebody closed it. I want to know why."

"I don't really care," Meat admitted.

"Maybe there was something on that page that would give us a clue to the murderer."

Meat could hear the sound of the heavy book being opened, then the rustling of pages being turned.

This was the one thing he didn't like about Herculeah: that she was completely unaware of the fact that other people—perfectly normal people like himself—had perfectly normal fears. Here they were in a house where a woman had been murdered—brutally murdered, the TV newscaster had said. The stains were probably still on the floor and—

At that moment he heard something. The sound of a footstep on the stairs above.

Meat couldn't move. He couldn't breathe. His heart began to thud unhealthily in his chest.

His head had been slumped forward over his knees, and he now found he was unable to lift it. He was frozen with fear. The best he could do was to roll his eyes upward and watch the stairs.

He saw nothing. This made him more afraid. And he found, as the seconds passed, that the longer he saw nothing, the more afraid he became.

Silence.

Silence.

Step.

Silence.

Silence.

Meat knew he should warn Herculeah, but his voice had departed with his ability to move. He understood how deer and rabbits became frozen with fear, even when they might get away if they ran.

Step.

From the parlor, Herculeah called, "It's too bad I didn't notice what page the book was opened to when I first came in the room. That would really help. I know it was in the middle, and I know there was a picture on it. The trouble is, there's a picture on almost every page."

Step.

"I don't know why," Herculeah continued, happily unaware of the danger, "but I just have the feeling I'll know it when I come to it. Maybe my amulet is bringing me luck. I still have it on, by the way. And you know what I've decided? That I'm never going to open it. I'm going to keep the good luck inside. Because what if I did open it and a piece of old, chewed chewing gum or something equally gross fell out? Believe me, Meat, a lot of luck comes from just feeling lucky. And right now I feel lucky." This was followed by the sound of vigorous page turning.

Meat had never felt less lucky in his life. His eyes were rolled up so far into his head they might never come down.

Now he saw it: a foot.

He couldn't tell in the faint moonlight whether it was a man's foot or a woman's. It didn't matter. It was the scariest foot he had ever seen in his life. He had not known a foot could be so terrifying.

He wanted to scream. He wanted to run for his life. He wanted to disappear.

He did the next best thing. His eyes continued their painful roll up into his head.

Meat fainted.

17

VOODOO DOLLS AND ALL THAT JAZZ

"Well, this is really frustrating," Herculeah continued as she studied the book. "I know there's something important on one of these two pages, and I cannot figure out what it is."

There was no answer from the hallway.

"I held the book up, and I let it fall open on its own. Sometimes, Meat, books open to the exact place you want them to. It's like the book has its own intelligence. It knows what you want and it helps you." She gave a little laugh at herself. "Maybe I think that because I love books so much, but I really feel that's what has happened here."

Still no answer from the hallway.

"But you know what else I'm wondering? Maybe the book was closed for another reason, something I haven't even considered. Did you ever think of that?" When he still didn't answer, she called, "Meat, are you listening to me?"

She heard the sound of a footstep in the hall.

"Well, at least I know you're alive."

Again no answer.

"I wish you'd come look at this page and see if anything rings a bell. It's a page about, well, voodoo dolls and fetishes and all that jazz. You know the stuff I'm talking about. A doll stands for a person and, like, you stick a pin in it and the person dies." She paused. "Are you listening to me, or what?"

This time when there was no answer, Herculeah turned from the table. "Meat?"

Herculeah gasped. She gripped the edge of the table for support. The flashlight slipped from her hand and fell with a thud to the carpet.

Madame Rosa stood in the doorway in her black cloak. The hood was pulled over her head, hiding her face.

Outwardly Herculeah did not move. Inwardly she shrank back in horror.

There was a long moment while they faced each other in the darkness. The only light was from the

moonlit window behind the figure and from the flashlight at Herculeah's feet.

The nightmare seemed to stretch and grow. It became almost a living thing.

Herculeah blinked, and the moment snapped. She
knew what had happened. Herculeah exploded.

"Meat, now that is not one bit funny! You actually
scared me. I'm spooked enough being right here
where Madame Rosa died without you adding to it by
pretending to be her. Now, take that cape off. I mean
it. Now!"

From the hood of the cloak came one word.
"Herculeah."

The voice was faint, and somehow faraway, but it
was Madame Rosa's voice. Other people could imitate
the way she spoke, but this was Madame Rosa's voice.

Herculeah swallowed, and the sound was louder
than the voice had been.

"But, but—you're dead."

Again, just her name. "Herculeah."

"What are you doing here? What do you want?
Who are you?"

There was another pause, and then the voice said
one more word. "Tarot."

The figure took one step backward. "Tarot." The
cloak fluttered as if in a breeze.

Herculeah felt that the figure was leaving, and it

seemed important to keep her there, to find out who she was. Herculeah said, "Wait. I've got Tarot. He's at my house. I can go get him. Wait!"

She remembered the flashlight and bent quickly to retrieve it. When she looked up, the figure had disappeared.

Herculeah stood for a moment without moving. She sank into Madame Rosa's chair. She set the flashlight down on the table and pressed her hands to her face, rubbing her eyes as if she had seen something that could not be real.

She remembered Meat. She got up and walked as if in a dream toward the hall.

"Meat?" she asked. Her voice was too weak to be heard.

Meat was regaining consciousness.

He was still slumped forward, and his head had dropped between his knees, in the classic position for regaining consciousness, although that was not something Meat particularly wanted to do.

His eyes opened. They focused slowly on the old moonlit rug at his feet. It was not a familiar pattern, and for a moment he didn't know where he was. He felt dizzy again.

Then his mind began to clear. He remembered the terrible truth.

He was on a chair in Madame Rosa's hallway, and someone was slowly coming down the stairs.

He lifted his head. The person was no longer coming down the stairs. Where was he? Where was he?

His eyes shifted. Meat was proud that he did not gasp with horror. The person was now in the hallway! The person was standing at the bottom of the stairs. The person was by the coatrack!

Perhaps the fainting spell had refreshed him, for Meat suddenly got noiselessly to his feet. Even his knees didn't give their usual protesting pop.

He crouched forward, one hand on the floor. Then in a rush, head down, arms up, Meat started forward. It felt like a move Meat had seen in professional football, something he had never thought he himself could execute.

He caught the intruder unawares and had the pleasure of hearing him hit the floor and let out a tremendous grunt of shock and pain.

His sense of satisfaction lasted two seconds. After that came the realization that the intruder might get up, and Meat knew he did not have another professional football move in his body.

After that, came an even worse realization. The tremendous grunt of shock and pain that had given him such satisfaction had sounded a lot like Herculeah.

18

FOOT NIGHTMARES

"Look, I didn't do it on purpose," Meat said for the third time.

He and Herculeah were in Madame Rosa's hallway. Herculeah was still sitting on the floor, shining the flashlight on her arms and legs, checking for bruises. The jolt of being shoved headlong into a wall had temporarily put Madame Rosa out of Herculeah's mind.

"Then why did you do it?"

Now she shone the light up into Meat's face.

Meat shielded his eyes. "Don't do that, please. I have sensitive eyes."

"I have sensitive arms and legs, too, you know."

"I'm sorry about that."

"Then tell me why you did it."

"I told you. Why do I have to keep going over it? I was sitting here, and I heard a footstep overhead."

He swallowed thickly, remembering.

"Then I heard another footstep."

Again he had to swallow to continue.

"Then I saw a foot. It was the most terrible, the most frightening foot in the world. You probably don't think a single foot could be that terrifying—"

"I saw Madame Rosa's foot sticking out from under the table, remember?"

"Well, yes, but that foot was dead, and this one was living."

He closed his eyes, remembering, and mercifully Herculeah turned the flashlight away from his face. Possibly his face was too twisted with pain and fright to watch for any length of time.

"That's all I remember. I must have fainted from shock."

Herculeah was silent, and her silence, as usual, made Meat feel the need to defend himself.

"It was not a dream, Herculeah. I know you're going to say it was a dream. I know you're going to claim I fell asleep as usual. And I admit I have been known to fall asleep, but this was no dream. This was the realest thing that ever happened to me in my life. I will remember that foot until the day I die. I will have night-mares about that foot."

"Nightmares can seem very real," she said.

"Then when I came to"—Meat went on as if she had not spoken—"I was somehow filled with strength and purpose and I rushed forward and—I don't have to tell you what I did then."

"No, you don't. Help me up."

Meat pulled her to her feet. She brushed off the seat of her jeans.

"So did you find what you were looking for?" he asked.

"Not in the book."

"Well, at least you found out about the pictures."

"A very strange thing happened to me, Meat."

The tone of her voice sent shivers up his neck. He turned up the collar of his jacket.

"I'm not sure I want to hear this."

"You have to. This is how I know you're telling me the truth about someone coming down the stairs."

Now he was sure he was about to hear something he did not want to hear. But he couldn't stop his mouth from saying, "How?"

"I saw someone in the hall."

"Who?" There was such a long pause that he thought he hadn't been heard. He shouted, *Who?*

"Madame Rosa."

For a moment Meat thought he hadn't heard right. "Madame Rosa is dead!"

"Meat, she was standing right there where you are standing now."

Meat took an involuntary side step.

"I thought it was you playing a joke."

The thought of putting on Madame Rosa's cloak, even for a joke, caused Meat to shudder as if he had a chill.

"And I yelled at you that it wasn't funny and to stop it, and then she spoke."

"She said something?" This was an awed whisper. "She spoke?"

"She said my name. And you know how people are always imitating Madame Rosa? She has an easy voice to imitate. But this was her voice. It wasn't an imitation. It was her voice."

"Did she say anybody else's name?" Meat asked after a brief hesitation.

"Yes."

Another hesitation. "Mine?"

"No, she said, 'Tarot.' I even offered to go get him. I didn't want her to get away. Then I reached down for my flashlight—I wanted to see her—and when I stood up, she was gone."

Suddenly Meat's eyes widened.

"Give me that flashlight," he said.

Something in his voice made Herculeah hand him the light at once.

He turned the beam on the coatrack in the corner.

"Look," he said.

"At what?"

"Madame Rosa's cloak was there when I sat down and now—now it's gone."

Herculeah looked at Meat. "This was no dream."

"I know."

"Someone was here."

"But it couldn't have been Madame Rosa. You saw her body."

"You know what, Meat?" she said thoughtfully. "I saw her body, that's true. But I didn't actually see her face. That's what's making me wonder. Her hair had come loose and had fallen over her face. What if—"

There was a loud knock at the door. Herculeah and Meat instinctively drew closer together.

"Madame Rosa," Meat whispered, his voice deep with dread.

"More likely the police," Herculeah said.

Meat gasped, although only ten minutes ago he would have welcomed them.

"Herculeah, open this door," a voice demanded. "I know you're in there."

"It's my mom," Herculeah said. Now there was dread in her voice as well.

"I know you're in there. Open this door."

Herculeah moved to the front door. She unlocked it and pulled it open.

"I knew it!" her mother said. She strode into the hallway. "I knew it. You took that key the minute my back was turned."

"Mom, I can explain."

"And, Meat, is that you back there?"

"Yes'm." Meat stepped forward.

"Meat, you've got better sense than Herculeah. You should have stopped her."

"I did my best."

"Herculeah, this is trespassing!"

"Mom, listen. Someone was here. Someone was upstairs. And they came down. Meat heard them, didn't you, Meat?"

"And I saw them—the foot, anyway. And, Mrs. Jones, that was the most terrible foot there could be in the world. I'll probably have foot nightmares tonight. I know I will."

"And I saw the person. Mom, listen. It was either Madame Rosa or somebody pretending to be her. Oh, Mom, now that you're here, we can put on all the lights and really search."

Meat held up one hand as if to stop anyone from speaking.

"Did you hear that?"

"What?"

"It sounded like the click of the back door closing," Meat said in a hushed voice. "I think someone just went out the kitchen door."

"Great!" Herculeah said, turning in that direction. "If we hurry—"

"If we hurry," her mother said firmly, taking her arm, "we can get home before midnight. Come along, Meat."

Meat glanced anxiously toward the kitchen. "Gladly," he said.

19

THE OTHER HALF OF THE PICTURE

"So."

Herculeah always hated it when her father started a conversation like that.

"So."

Another one. Two "so"s. This was going to be bad.

"Your mom tells me you went back to Madame Rosa's last night."

It was Sunday, and Herculeah and her father were in the car, driving to an Atlanta Falcons football game.

Her father had spoken in a casual, conversational tone, but Herculeah was aware this was not going to be a casual chat. His profile was stern.

She said, "Mom told you that?"

"She did."

"I wish you and Mom wouldn't discuss me behind my back."

"I wish we didn't have to."

"So, what did Mom say?"

"She said she had taken the key away from you, and you got it out of her drawer and went over there, taking poor Meat along with you. It was a very dangerous thing to do."

"Actually Meat turned out to be the most dangerous part. He tackled me. You'd think he was—who's that big mean Falcon?"

"They're all big and mean."

"Well, that was the only time I was in any real danger. I got spooked, I admit that, when Madame Rosa appeared." She turned to her father. "Dad, are you convinced that body was Madame Rosa's?"

"Yes, I am."

"Well, I'm not."

"Listen, Herculeah, whoever killed Madame Rosa is still out there." He seemed to be choosing his words carefully. "This was not some random killing. This was not an intruder who killed and left town."

"I know. I remember you telling me that most murders are not committed by unknown assailants."

"That has been my experience."

"And this one?

"This one, too."

Herculeah hoped her father would elaborate, but he didn't, so she said, "You think it was someone Madame Rosa knew?"

"Yes."

"A relative? She told me she only had one of them still alive."

"It's a possibility."

"Meat thinks she was blackmailing people. That she'd find out all their secrets and blackmail them, but I don't think so. Do you?"

"It's a possibility."

"I did notice one interesting thing while I was in that house. This was one of the reasons I went in there. She had a lot of family pictures, and there was one of her with a boy. I'd seen it there a lot of times. Last night it was gone."

She glanced at her father, but he seemed intent on traffic.

"You don't suppose it could be the boy in the picture that killed her?"

"We haven't been able to locate any relatives."

Herculeah took in a quick breath. "The mime," she said.

"What?"

"The mime."

"Mime? You mean one of those white-faced people?"

"Yes. Dad, wouldn't it be the perfect disguise? I mean, we see the mime every day, but we don't know what he looks like or how old he is or anything. He could wash his face and come out, and nobody would even recognize him."

She leaned back with satisfaction. "Meat would be so pleased if it turned out to be the mime. He can't stand mimes." She laughed. "I'd love to see you try to interrogate a mime."

Her father's tight profile eased into a reluctant smile.

"Or see Judge Kellerman try."

A wider smile.

"I wish I knew what happened to that picture."

"Well, I don't guess there's any harm in my telling you we found it."

"You did?" She swiveled around. "Where?"

"Well, we found half of it. The Madame Rosa half. It was in the alley behind the house. The frame, some broken glass, and half the picture."

"That proves it was important, don't you think? That's it! The killer tore up the picture and took the half that could identify him!"

"Or he took the picture to make us think it could identify him."

"Were there any fingerprints?"

He shook his head.

"Of course not." She laughed. "The mime always wears gloves." She shook her head as if to make herself get serious. "I wish I knew where that mime lives. Maybe I ought to follow him."

"You're not following any mime. This is a dangerous business. Give me your word."

"Oh, all right, but you know what? I went into that house, got scared, got slammed into a wall, got Mom mad at me, got a lecture from you and"—she showed her empty hands—"and all for nothing!"

Herculeah glanced at her father's profile. His lips had tightened again, forming a straight line across his tanned face. She was sorry she had gotten the conversation back to her illegal entry into Madame Rosa's.

"I want you to make me another promise, hon."

"What, Dad?"

"I want you to promise you will not go back in that house."

"Oh, I'm happy to promise that. I don't want to go back. I really did get scared, if you want to know the truth. Anyway, there's nothing to go back for."

"There better not be."

20

DEAR ABBY

"I just did something I didn't think I would ever do in my whole life," Meat said as soon as Herculeah answered the phone.

"What?"

"I wrote a letter to Dear Abby."

"I bet I know what you said. 'There's a girl across the street from me that keeps getting me in trouble. How can I get her to stop?'"

"No. If you didn't keep getting me in trouble, my life would be a complete bust."

"Then what?"

"I wrote for information about finding my father.

Remember, you mentioned it last night when we were getting ready to trespass."

Herculeah gave the telephone a look of disgust at Meat's choice of words. Then she smiled. "I can't wait to hear what she says. You know, I have only learned one pleasant thing since this terrible mess started."

"What?"

"That you have a dancing father."

"Well, so Madame Rosa said. She could be wrong."

"I wonder what kind of dancing. Toe? Tap? The twist? Boogie?"

"Don't try to be funny. I do not appreciate jokes where my father is concerned."

"Sorry."

Herculeah was on the sofa. She stretched out to get more comfortable. "I went to the Falcons game with my dad today. I just got back. We were going to stop for supper, but my dad got a call."

"I saw you come in."

As Meat spoke, he remembered seeing them leave as well. He had stood at the window, jealously watching as they drove away. If he had a father, he would even be willing to go to a Falcons football game to be with him.

"I pumped my dad for information, but I didn't get much. During the game . . . to be honest, sometimes football bores me, but I don't want my dad to know, because he does not bore me. I like to be with him. Anyway, during the game I started recreating Madame Rosa's last hours."

"Oh?"

"Here's what I think." Herculeah sat up straight, caught up in her theory. "Madame Rosa had been reading something in that book, and she goes into the kitchen to boil some water, possibly for tea. She drank a lot of herbal tea. I drank one cup once, which was enough for me. The doorbell rings. Or maybe it doesn't. Maybe the killer just walks in. That's more like it. Madame Rosa is back in the kitchen and she hears Tarot screech, 'Beware! Beware!' and she knows someone has come into the house. I'm getting goose-bumps, are you?"

"No," Meat lied.

"Madame Rosa is so upset, she doesn't even turn off the stove. She goes into the hall. Nobody there. She goes into the living room. Nobody there. She goes into the parlor. There he is—the killer."

"There he is!" Meat said.

"That's just what I said."

"No, I mean the mime! There he is! Look out your window."

"Oh, he's probably been to the flea market. It's seven o'clock, so it just closed."

"Let's follow him."

"I can't. I promised my dad I wouldn't."

"Well, I didn't promise."

"Meat, my dad feels like this is dangerous. I'm beginning to think so, too."

"Well, all right, I won't follow him. I'll just take a walk in the same direction he's walking in, and see where he goes."

"Meat! That is following! Just like us going into that house was trespassing and—"

But Meat had hung up the phone.

Herculeah pressed against the window and watched as Meat came out of his house, pulling on his jacket. He ran down the steps.

Herculeah hesitated.

She reached for her binoculars. She raised them to her eyes. She noticed three things:

1. The mime had paused at a store window.

2. The mime was checking to see if he was being followed.

3. Meat was busy zipping up his jacket and wasn't aware the mime knew Meat was following him.

Herculeah put down the binoculars.

"I promised my dad that I wouldn't follow the mime. I did not promise my dad that I wouldn't follow Meat."

She reached for her jacket and headed for the door.

21

MEAT AND MIME

Meat paused at the corner. He peered around the drugstore. The mime was halfway down the block.

Just the sight of that black suit, those white-gloved hands caused Meat to shiver. He took a deep breath. He squared his shoulders. He turned the corner, prepared to duck into the nearest doorway if necessary.

It wasn't. The sidewalk was empty. The mime had disappeared.

Slowly, looking from side to side, exactly as Herculeah had imitated him doing at the flea market, Meat continued down the sidewalk.

The last place he had seen the mime was just before

the entrance to the alley that ran between the houses. No one used the alley much anymore, and it was overgrown with weeds.

Meat stopped and peered into the alley. The dark shadows from the buildings made it even more uninviting. Still, he knew the mime had to have gone this way.

He glanced around uneasily. No one was in sight. He lifted his hand and waved, as if to a friend in front of the drugstore. If the mime was watching—and he probably was—this would make the mime think someone had seen Meat entering the alley and make the mime think twice about . . . whatever.

Meat walked slowly into the alley. Gravel and broken glass crunched beneath his feet.

He passed an old sagging garage, and the rotten boards gave off the smell of mildew and rot. He put his hand over his face to blot out the smell. Meat was sensitive to odors.

He peered around the back of the garage, and in one terrible gasp, he inhaled a deep breath of the air he had wanted to avoid. He was face-to-face with the mime.

Meat coughed up some of the air. Then he managed to say, "Hi."

The mime gave an elaborate gesture that asked, or so it seemed to Meat, the question he most didn't want to answer: Why are you following me?

"I wasn't. I just happened to be, you know, coming this way."

Then, to Meat's unhappiness, there followed a dreadful one-sided conversation, apparently the only kind you can have with a mime.

The mime: I don't like to be followed.

"No, no, that's why I wasn't following you. I don't follow people."

The mime: What do you want?

"Nothing. Nothing. I don't want one single thing."

The mime: Then why are you here?

"I don't know. Actually, I was just getting ready to go."

As Meat peered into the white face, it almost seemed like one of those death masks you see in museums. The mime's face was still empty of expression, but Meat had the feeling that the mime was mad enough to commit some sort of murderous act upon him. He remembered that wave he had been clever enough to make to his nonexistent friend, and he added, "My friend's waiting in front of the drugstore."

He took two backward steps toward the street.

"Actually," he said then, surprising himself, "this friend-in-front-of-the-drugstore"—he made one word of it—"and I are looking into Madame Rosa's murder. We're beginning to think that the murderer was a young man, someone from the neighborhood."

The mime waited.

"He might be someone whose mother had consulted Madame Rosa. The mother was afraid of the son. He'd threatened her with a knife—"

At that, the mime threw back his head and laughed. And he didn't just pantomime laughter. He roared.

The effect was so startling that Meat moved back some more.

"I'm sorry, but that tears me up," the mime said.

Meat shrugged. Now the tables had turned, and it was the mime who spoke and Meat who was wordless.

"You must not know my mom."

Meat shook his head.

"In about a minute you will."

They waited in silence, then the back door of the house was thrown open. A loud voice yelled, "Bertram, you out there?"

"Yes, Mom."

"Well, get yourself in here. Supper's ready. I mean now."

"Yes, Mom."

The mime looked at Meat. "That woman has never been afraid of anything or anybody in her whole life."

Meat nodded. "I can believe that." He lifted one hand in farewell.

He walked down the alley and met Herculeah in

front of the drugstore. "This is exactly where you were supposed to be," Meat said.

"I followed you. I saw the mime glance in a store window. He knew you were following him, and I was worried."

"Well, you don't have to worry anymore."

"Why not?"

"Not about the mime anyway. The mime's mother did not consult Madame Rosa. The mime's mother isn't afraid of anything."

They started for home together.

As they walked, Herculeah said, "I think we're overlooking one very important thing."

"What's that?"

"Madame Rosa saw something at the flea market that really scared her."

"Yeah, scared her to death," Meat said.

"Tell me what that man said again."

Meat thought for a moment. "I'm not sure it will be word for word."

"That's okay."

"He said she came running out 'like the devil himself was after her.' Those were his exact words. Then he said he stopped her. He asked if she needed help. He said she was as white as if she'd seen a ghost. She muttered something about a knife, and he asked if somebody had pulled a knife on her. She gave him a look he said he'd never forget. Then she said, 'No, but they will.'"

They walked to the end of the block in silence.

Meat glanced at Herculeah. He said, "Maybe we ought to go back to the flea market and talk to the man again, try to find out what happened."

"I don't have to," Herculeah said. "I think I already know."

22

MADAME ROSA CALLS

The phone rang.

Herculeah crossed to her mother's desk and picked it up. It was after office hours, but sometimes clients called her mother at night.

"Mim Jones's office," she said.

There was a silence.

"Mim Jones's office."

Again there was no answer, but for some reason Herculeah did not hang up. She waited. She could hear soft breathing on the other end of the line. It made her uneasy and yet she still could not make herself hang up.

After another long moment, a faint, hauntingly familiar voice said her name, "Herculeah." It was a voice from another world, a voice from the dead.

For a moment Herculeah couldn't speak. Now it was her quickened breathing that went over the line.

This was the voice Herculeah had heard that night in the hallway. In her mind she again saw the cloaked figure.

When she was finally able to speak, she said, "This is Herculeah."

There was another pause. Herculeah knew the caller had something more to say. All she had to do was wait.

"This is Madame Rosa."

Although that was what Herculeah had expected, she found herself shaking her head in disbelief. She reminded herself that Madame Rosa had a voice that was easily copied, that this couldn't be her. Madame Rosa was dead. But the voice on the phone did not sound like an imitation. It sounded like Madame Rosa herself.

She forced herself to speak. "I don't believe you. Who are you really?"

"I tell the truth. I am Madame Rosa."

"No. Madame Rosa is dead," Herculeah said in a flat voice, as if to remind herself. "I was the one who found the body. I saw you."

"You saw a dead woman. I grant you that."

Herculeah waited.

"But the dead woman was not me."

Herculeah exploded. "It was. I saw you, saw her. Your shoes, your long hair, your—"

"But did you take a really good look. Did you?" A pause. "I thought not. Did you lift the hair and look at the face?"

"No."

"If you didn't see the face, how can you be so sure?"

"It had to be you. I know it was. My father said it was, and he's with the police."

"The police, they can be mistaken like everybody else. The body that you saw was that of my sister."

"I don't believe you."

"My sister, Marianna. Is true."

"I don't believe it."

"Is it so hard for you to believe I am alive? I'm your friend." The voice was wheedling now. "You should be happy your friend is alive."

"I don't know who you are, but you're not my friend. I'm hanging up and calling the police."

"Wait. Give me one minute. I tell you what happened. One minute is all I ask. Then you hang up all you want to. Call anybody you want. Police. Anybody."

Herculeah hesitated.

"You are still there, Herculeah?"

"Yes."

"You will listen?"

"I'll listen, but—"

"That day, that terrible day, someone come to my house. He come to kill me, but my sister was there. My sister and I just alike—long hair, long noses. My sister opened the door.

"The man never give my sister a chance to say she not Madame Rosa. Or maybe she say it, and he don't believe."

There was a pause.

"And whoever kill my sister—Herculeah, believe this—whoever kill my sister, when he find out it is her dead and not me, he will come after me."

Herculeah lowered herself into her mother's chair.

"This time there won't be a sister to give her life for me. This time he will succeed. This time he kill me. You want that to happen?"

Herculeah could not answer.

"I have to get away. I don't want to die, Herculeah. Don't let your friend die!"

The rising desperation in Madame Rosa's voice gave Herculeah a feeling of desperation, too.

"But why are you calling me? What can I do? Why don't you call the police?"

"The police." Her tone was scornful. "The police cannot help in matters like this."

"Yes, they can. My father would help you in a minute."

"Your fadda cannot help me." Her voice lowered. "Only you." It was a plea.

"But what can I do? I can't do anything. My parents are furious at me already. I had to promise never to go in your house again."

"The house." More scorn. "You don't need to come in the house. I wouldn't ask you to do anything against your parents."

"What then?"

When Madame Rosa spoke again, her voice was almost businesslike.

"You have Tarot."

"Yes."

"You have him at your house."

"Yes."

"Then, it is simple. You know I will not leave without Tarot. He has been with me since I was a little girl of four. Even if the murderer find me and kill me, I not leave without my Tarot. That's all that I want you to do. Bring me Tarot."

"Why don't you come get him?"

"I show my face on this street, I am as good as dead. You will bring, yes?"

"Where are you?" Herculeah asked.

"I am in back of my house. I have packed my things.

I am ready. You come, bring Tarot, and I am on my way."

"But—"

"I beg of you. Just this one last favor, and I am out of your life forever. I beg you, I beg you. I wait for you, Herculeah. Please help me. Do not fail me now."

And the line went dead.

23

THE BLACK ROBE

Herculeah dialed Meat's line. "Busy," she said to herself. She glanced out the window at his house.

She waited. She dialed again. "Get off the phone. I need you!"

She made a decision, put down the phone, and quickly climbed the stairs to her room. She stood for a moment in her doorway.

Tarot was on his stand by the window. He cocked his head and looked at her.

"Beware! Beware!" he said.

"I wish you knew some other words."

Herculeah sighed, pulled herself from the doorway,

and crossed the room. Her head was full of questions. Was Marianna the living relative Madame Rosa had mentioned? And what of the sister's son? Was he living? Nothing made sense. That was why she wanted to see Madame Rosa—or find out who was pretending to be her.

"Come on, Tarot. Let's go."

She put the bird on her shoulder. "I've got to get Meat to go with us. I called his house, but the line was busy. I'll try again before we leave. He won't want to come. He hates that house. I do, too, but—"

Tarot's wing brushed her cheek as he flapped. The air he stirred around her face smelled of feathers and dry seeds.

"If Meat doesn't answer, I'm going to stop by his house. Then the three of us are going to Madame Rosa's. I thought she was dead, but now I don't know. I wish my mom was home. I would call Dad, but it's his poker night, and I don't know where they're playing. If all she wants is the parrot . . ."

Herculeah dialed Meat's phone number. Still busy. She hung up the phone and went out the front door. She crossed the street and knocked on Meat's door. Meat's mother opened it and stepped back with a gasp.

"What are you doing with that awful bird?" she asked. "It's that woman's bird, isn't it, that witch? I recognize it. Get it off my porch. I won't have that bird anywhere near me."

"Is Meat home?"

"No, I am happy to say Albert is not at home. He's not at home, so you can't get him in any more trouble."

"Do you know when he'll be back?"

"If I knew, I wouldn't tell you."

Meat's mother turned her head to the side and looked at Herculeah from under her heavy brows. "Are you in some kind of trouble?"

"I don't know. I don't think so. Maybe."

"Well, I can't stand here talking all night. I'm on the phone. Long distance."

"Tell Meat I came by. Tell him . . ."

Meat's mother closed the door before Herculeah could think of a message, and Herculeah went down the stairs. She took them one by one, hesitantly, as if she didn't want to proceed.

With these same slow steps, she walked down the sidewalk. She paused at Madame Rosa's gate. Herculeah had a deep feeling of dread, of something about to happen.

"Madame Rosa," she called at the gate.

There was no answer.

The house was dark. It had an empty, deserted look,

as if whoever had lived here had left a thousand years ago, instead of a few days ago.

Herculeah pushed open the gate. She glanced over her shoulder, remembering that when she and Meat had entered, a police car had cruised by. Unfortunately, there was no police car tonight.

Herculeah left the gate open behind her. Keeping away from the shrubbery, she made her way to the side of the house.

"Get ready, Tarot, because when I see her, I'm throwing you in her direction and taking off. Madame Rosa?"

No answer.

"Madame Rosa."

Herculeah took a few steps around the side of the house.

"I am here."

Herculeah turned. The figure had come out of the shrubbery behind Herculeah, cutting off Herculeah's exit to the street.

"I've got the parrot," she said in a rush.

She could see a black-robed figure in the small patch of moonlight that filtered through the old trees, but she couldn't see the face. Her heart began to pound in her chest.

"Yes, I see. You have the bird."

Herculeah paused, judging the distance, the time it would take to rush past this black figure.

"Come, bring him to me."

Herculeah moved sideways. The bird fluttered on her shoulder, and Herculeah put up one hand to calm him.

In that moment, Tarot saw the figure against the shrubbery. He screeched, "Beware! Beware!" and beat his wings furiously.

Herculeah froze. She knew that Tarot never cried "beware" to Madame Rosa, only to strangers.

And Herculeah knew that whoever it was coming toward her wrapped in Madame Rosa's cloak, it was not Madame Rosa.

24

THE KNIFE

Herculeah stepped back. On her shoulder, Tarot's talons clutched, pinching her flesh. His wings beat anxiously against her face.

"Who—who are you?" Herculeah asked. Her voice trembled. Her throat was dry.

"I tell you. Madame Rosa."

"No."

There was a pause.

"Madame Ro-sa," the voice said again, this time in a sly, teasing way that turned Herculeah's blood cold.

"Your voice is like hers," Herculeah admitted, forcing herself to talk normally. "You might fool me, but you can't fool the parrot."

"Who knows about a bird? Maybe in the darkness, Tarot get confused. Maybe he make a mistake, as I said, like the police."

"No, you are not Madame Rosa."

There was a pause and then a different voice, a man's voice, spoke.

"No, unfortunately for you, I am not Madame Rosa."

"Well, you're somebody who knows Madame Rosa very well," Herculeah continued in a rush.

"Yes, I knew her."

Herculeah began to inch sideways toward the fence. She went on in a deliberate conversational tone, "Because you imitate her voice perfectly, and you couldn't do that if you didn't know her."

Herculeah stopped. She drew in a breath. "Or maybe," she said slowly, "maybe you're somebody who knows how to imitate voices."

"That could be."

"Maybe you're someone who makes a living imitating voices."

As Herculeah said that, she was back at the flea market, standing in front of the puppet show, listening to dozens of different voices, all from one man.

"Now you're getting smart."

Herculeah said, "Frankie." It was not a guess, not a question. "The puppeteer."

He did not answer, but Herculeah knew she had hit the mark.

"You killed Madame Rosa."

No answer.

"I want to know why. I have to know why."

Herculeah continued to move sideways. Just two feet more and she could rush the figure in the cloak, knock him down, head for the street. With any luck she could be over the fence and—

Her thoughts broke off. It was important to keep talking.

"I really do want to know why. I don't think anybody cares but me. You did kill her, didn't you?"

"Yes."

The voice seemed closer. Perhaps the puppeteer was inching in her direction as she was moving toward the fence. She couldn't see him clearly now.

She stepped on a dried twig and the snap caused Tarot to beat his wings again. "Beware! Beware!"

"It was your mother who consulted Madame Rosa, wasn't it?"

"Yes." He gave a dry laugh. "I used to scare my mom into doing what I wanted. My mom would give me grief over something, and I'd start playing with a kitchen knife, twirling it on the counter or holding it like this."

Now Herculeah could see the glint of a knife in his hand. He had drawn a knife from under his cloak. He was raising it.

Herculeah knew he had stabbed one person. He wouldn't hesitate to stab another.

She swallowed. She barely managed to say, "Go on with what you were saying."

"I guess I scared her maybe a little too much—like I'm scaring you."

"I'm not afraid."

"You should be." Another of those dry, frightening laughs. "Well, my mother was. She went to consult the famous Madame Rosa. 'Oh, Madame Rosa, I'm afraid of my son. Is he going to kill me, Madame, yes or no? Is my little Frankie going to kill me?'"

Now he was speaking in his mother's voice. Herculeah was cold with fear and dread. She felt as if she were in Madame Rosa's parlor with the frightened mother and Madame Rosa, actually hearing the conversation.

"'Give me something of his. Bring me something.'"

"'I could bring you the knife he threatens me with.'"

The terrible two-part conversation continued, with the puppeteer taking both parts.

"'I'll go home right now and get the knife. You'll wait for me, Madame Rosa?'"

"'I wait. . . .'

"'I am back. Here, here is the knife my boy threatens me with. Here take it. Tell me.'

"'Yes. Yes. Your boy, he kill with this knife. Your boy will kill!'"

In his own voice the puppeteer added, "I guess the old broad actually flipped out, fainted. My mom told me about it when she got home. She said, 'Frankie, she thinks you're going to kill.' I said, 'Mom, I'm no killer. You know that. I'll handle it.' I meant to handle it by scaring Madame Rosa."

Herculeah took another step toward the fence. In the darkness, the puppeteer did, too.

"I made a witch puppet. You saw her."

"Yes. And just as I thought, it was modeled after Madame Rosa."

"Of course, even down to the cloak." He gave a flourish that made the cloak flutter around him. On Herculeah's shoulder, Tarot gave an answering flutter.

"Oh, I enjoyed that play. Madame Rosa was doing her little palm-reading thing across the way, and she looked up and there she was on the puppet stage. Her face. Her voice. Her cloak. My knife.

"She froze with her mouth open—was too scared to close it, I guess—until the witch got stabbed."

"That's when she fled?"

"I thought she got the message. Then the old fool

went to your mom, a private detective, and I didn't like that. I knew I had to really scare the old woman—like I'm scaring you."

"I'm n-not afraid."

"A-aren't you?" the puppeteer asked. This time he spoke in Herculeah's voice.

"Go on with your story," she managed to say.

"I went to her house. I opened the door with the knife—such useful things." Beneath his hood he smiled. "Madame Rosa was in the kitchen. I was just going to put the knife somewhere so she could find it. There was a big book on the table. I decided to stick the knife in that. It fell open to a page on dolls. Voodoo dolls. I liked that. It fit. Dolls. Puppets. I raised my knife. Right then that stupid bird woke up and yelled, 'Beware!'

"Madame Rosa came in and she went crazy. I just wanted to scare her—that's all I was going to do—but she threw herself at me. She was going to tear my eyes out or something. She was a wild woman. And I was holding the knife like this—"

Again Herculeah saw the glint of metal.

"And she fell against it. I never wanted to kill her. I don't want to kill anybody. I don't want to kill you."

Herculeah took another step sideways.

"It just happened then, like it's going to happen now. She knew too much. You do, too."

Without any more warning, he came toward her. His long billowing cape made him seem huge. Herculeah threw Tarot at him. There was a flurry of wings and cape as the puppeteer fought off the bird.

He managed to throw the bird to the ground. He came for Herculeah again. He made one thrust with the knife. He missed. He drew back for another.

She ducked and as she swirled away, she shoved him with all her strength. He stepped backward, stumbled on the hem of the cape, and fell to the ground.

This was the moment Herculeah had hoped for. She rushed past him. She had a moment of elation. She was free. She was going to get away. She was safe.

And then she felt his long, cold fingers circle her ankle.

25

WEAPON OF CHOICE

Herculeah cried out in fear. She kicked, trying to shake off his fingers, but the puppeteer's grip was strong. His fingers held.

She kicked again—and again. He was as desperate as she. They were both fighting for their lives.

Herculeah twisted. With her free foot she stomped down, hitting the puppeteer's wrist. There was a grunt of pain, but he held her fast.

Tarot, frantic with alarm, was flapping around Herculeah's legs, adding to the confusion, raising her fear. She glanced down.

In the moonlight she saw the knife in the puppeteer's free hand. She saw him draw it back. He was ready to strike.

Herculeah stomped again, this time with all her considerable strength. And this time there was a real scream and this time the fingers lost their grip.

Herculeah took off. She ran around the house, across the old lawn. She took the fence in one jump and kept running. She flew across the street.

As she came up on the pavement, she ran straight into something that knocked her breath out. It felt like a frying pan.

"Help me! Help me!" she gasped. She clutched the person who held it. "Help me! There's a man back there—a murderer. He tried to murder me, and he did murder Madame Rosa. He's got a knife. He may be coming—"

She broke off and glanced in fear over her shoulder. The street behind her was deserted. "He's—" She sagged, completely out of breath. Anyway, it was impossible to explain what had happened to a stranger.

"I knew you were going to get yourself into trouble," the woman Herculeah was clinging to said. "As soon as I saw that bird on your shoulder I knew no good would come of it."

This was not a stranger. Herculeah looked up. Lit by the streetlight was the surprisingly beautiful face of Meat's mother.

"Am I going to need this frying pan, or are you safe?"

"I think we're going to need more than that. We need the police."

"I already called them. I hung up on my sister—long distance from Chicago. I said, 'I got to hang up, Tiff.' I said, 'That was a girl at my door, and she had a bird on her shoulder that gets people in trouble. I'm calling the police.'"

"I'm glad you did. Oh, it was just awful. I can't describe it. I thought I was going to get away, and then I felt his hand grab my ankle—like that." She made a claw of her hand and shuddered at the memory. "It was the puppeteer."

Meat's mother went back to her original topic. "And as soon as I hung up after talking to the police, I went to the kitchen. My frying pan was waiting for me on the stove. I came out here and stopped on this very spot. I told myself I wasn't going to cross the street again unless I absolutely had to. I wasn't going a step closer to that murder house until I heard screams."

"I did scream." Herculeah thought that Meat's mother and her frying pan, her weapon of choice, would have been a welcome sight.

"Not loud enough. You have to work on your screams if you expect me to hear you."

"I will. But the puppeteer screamed, too. Didn't you hear him?"

"I wouldn't lift my frying pan for the likes of him," Meat's mother said firmly. She looked up. "Well, here they come at last."

A police car, blue lights flashing, siren wailing, came around the corner and stopped at the streetlight. A second car came racing around the back road, blocking off the alley.

"It's about time," Meat's mother told the first officer who got out of the car.

26

LIVING UP TO HERCULEAH

Herculeah was still standing with Meat's mother across the street from Madame Rosa's.

"We ought to go in the house," Meat's mother said. "It's cold. You're shivering."

"I'm not shivering from the cold."

"Come on. Let's go inside."

"I can't, yet. I want to see them bring him out. I have to be sure they got him. I'm really afraid of him. I won't sleep tonight unless I see him in custody."

They waited side by side under the streetlight.

"Well, there he is," Meat's mother said. "Take a good look."

The puppeteer came out between two policemen. He was no longer wearing Madame Rosa's cape, and he was in handcuffs. As the policeman put him in the back of the squad car, Herculeah caught a glimpse of his face. He no longer looked frightening. He looked frightened.

"Doesn't look as dangerous as I thought he would," Meat's mother said.

"When he was holding that knife, he looked dangerous."

"Looks can fool you sometimes."

Herculeah nodded. "Voices, too. I actually believed he was Madame Rosa." A sudden thought caused her to draw in her breath. "Oh, I'm going to have to go back for Tarot."

"That awful bird. I went over to Madame Rosa's one time—I needed to give her a piece of my mind about something—and the bird flew off its perch like it was trying to attack me. Maybe that wasn't its intention, but one of its claws got caught in my necklace. Fortunately, I wasn't wearing my pearls. I had on some cheerful plastic things I won at Bingo. If they hadn't been pop-it beads, they would have been ruined."

Meat's mother stuck her frying pan under her arm, since it obviously was not going to be needed. She sighed.

That sigh told Herculeah they were getting ready to talk about something more serious than pop-it beads.

"I wish I understood why this terrible murder happened," Meat's mother said.

"It happened, I think, because a boy tried to scare his mother," Herculeah said.

"Scare his own mother?"

"Yes."

"Well, thank goodness my Albert doesn't do that."

"No, you have a wonderful son." Herculeah broke off. "Oh, there's my mom. She'll help me now. Thank you very, very much."

"Just stay out of trouble. That will be thanks enough."

"I will."

"And keep my Albert out of trouble, too."

Herculeah waited for the squad car to pull away. Then she walked over to her mother's car and stood there impatiently.

"What was that police car doing here? There hasn't been another murder, has there?"

"No," Herculeah said, "but almost. The victim this time would have been me." She put her arms around her mother. "I am so glad to see you."

"What happened?" Her mother drew back to take a better look at Herculeah.

"Well, I got this telephone call and—"

There was a whine from the backseat of the car. "What's that noise?" Herculeah asked, bending down to peer into the rear window. She looked at her mother in amazement. "Mom, it's a dog. You've got a dog. Why? You have never liked dogs."

"I like them even less now. Remember I told you about that couple who were divorcing and one of them kidnapped the dog? Well, nothing would do but I had to get the dog back—which I did. Now, would you believe it, nobody wants the dog. They never did. They were just using him to fight over. See if you can get him out of the car, Herculeah. His name is Trip."

Herculeah looked at the dog in the backseat. He was a large yellow ball of misery, curled up, trembling with the indignity of being kidnapped and abandoned.

"Come on, Trip," Herculeah said in a kind voice. As she bent down, her knees began to shake again. "Mom, my knees won't stop shaking. Oh, I've got to tell you this one thing. It can't wait. The puppeteer killed Madame Rosa!"

"Who's the puppeteer?"

"Oh, Mom."

"Well, get this dog out of the car, and I'll listen to the whole thing."

"Come on, Trip," Herculeah urged. "Come on."

Trip rolled his eyes in Herculeah's direction but would not get out of the car.

"Come on! I haven't got all night." She turned to her mother. "Mom, he won't get out of the car. And the parrot's still loose in Madame Rosa's backyard. We have to catch him. He can't stay out all night. He'll freeze."

"What, may I ask, is the parrot doing in Madame Rosa's backyard. And who, may I ask, took him there? What has been going on here?"

"You aren't going to like it."

"I believe that."

"Anyway, it's too long to explain right now. Let's go get the parrot, then let's get the dog out of the car, then let's go in and call Dad and let him yell at us, and then we'll talk."

But before they did any of those things, they stood for a moment in the light from the streetlight. Herculeah's mother put her arm around Herculeah again.

"Sometimes," her mother said, "sometimes I wish I'd been watching another movie the night you were born."

"Instead of *Hercules vs the Moloch*?"

"Yes. I remember in the delivery room, I told the nurse that if you were a boy, I was going to name you Hercules. She tried to talk me out of it. She said if you were puny, the kids would tease you. Then the doctor got into the act. He said if you were a girl, I should name you Samsonya—for Samson. He even sang it like a Russian."

Herculeah's mother gave an imitation of the doctor's song. "'Oh, Samson-ya.'" She smiled. "The nurse did her best to talk me out of Herculeah. I sometimes wish I had listened to her."

"Why? I like my name."

"Because, my darling daughter, you are beginning to live up to it."

27

HERCULEAH AND THE GOLDEN FLEECE

"I've been trying to call you all night," Meat complained, "and your line's been busy. Who were you talking to for so long?"

"My dad."

Herculeah was lying in bed, her phone propped on the pillow. "My dad spent almost an hour giving me grief—unfairly! He said, 'You gave me your solemn promise, young lady, that you would not go inside Madame Rosa's house again.' I said, 'I didn't go inside the house. I only went in the yard.' But he pretended he couldn't see the difference. Sometimes my dad is very dense for a detective."

Meat said, with a certain sadness in his voice, "I can't believe I missed the whole thing. I was at the library."

"I wish I'd missed it," Herculeah answered. "My knees won't quit shaking. Well, every now and then they do, and then I remember the puppeteer's fingers around my ankle, and they start shaking again."

"I would have gone with you, Herculeah."

"I know that."

"Even though I had promised my mother, and myself, never to go back to that house again, I would have gone. I tackled him once, you know."

"That was me you tackled."

"Well, I thought it was him. That's what counts."

Herculeah leaned back on the pillow. "Oh, guess what my dad told me—after he stopped yelling at me, that is."

"I'm not that good at guessing."

"He told me they found Madame Rosa's one living relative. It's a sister, only her name's not Marianna, it's Sophie, and she lives in Duluth. Now comes the really good news."

"Oh?" Meat was suspicious. He knew that his idea of good news was usually not the same as Herculeah's.

"The sister's afraid of birds, so I get to keep Tarot—permanently!"

"Oh." Meat's suspicion was confirmed.

Herculeah continued without pause. "Meat, do you remember a conversation we had about a month ago?"

"I remember all our conversations," Meat answered.

"This one took place over the phone. It was late at night, and you had called to tell me there was an all-night Hercules party on TV and they were showing *Hercules vs the Moloch*."

"Yes, the Moloch was a man in a cat mask."

"I know. Then you said that the next movie was *Hercules vs the Hydra*, remember?"

"Yes, the Hydra was better. It was a many-headed monster."

"Exactly! That's the whole point!"

"I think I missed it."

"Well, that night, when you said Hydra, I got this funny feeling, a premonition, that my next challenge would be the Hydra. It didn't make sense then, but it does now."

"I still don't get it."

"The puppeteer was a many-headed monster."

There was a silence while Meat digested the information. "I guess you could say that." He paused, then added, "So do you have any premonition about what your next challenge is going to be?"

She laughed. "With the dog my mother brought home, maybe my next challenge will be the Golden Fleas."

"The Golden Fleece? But that's not Hercules. It's *Jason* and the Golden Fleece. Or did you say fleas? Golden fleas?"

"Yes, fleas. It was just a joke."

There was a silence. Then Herculeah said thoughtfully, "Actually, I do have a sort of premonition, but it doesn't make sense."

"What?"

"It happened when my mother and I were making a bed for Trip in the kitchen. He wouldn't get on the blanket, just kept looking at the stairs, like he wanted to sleep up there with us. My mom said, 'Don't give me that dog-in-the-manger look. You're sleeping in the kitchen,' and before I could explain to mom that she probably meant hangdog look, I got the premonition."

"So your premonition has something to do with a dog," Meat said thoughtfully.

"No, the manger! That's what doesn't make any sense. It's about the manger. I don't even think there are mangers anymore."

"A manger. Wait a minute. That does make sense! Herculeah, it does! A manger is in a stable, right? And one of Hercules' labors was cleaning the Aegean stable. I know I'm right about that, because I looked up Hercules in the encyclopedia one time—this was right after I met you—and it listed all of his labors."

"Cleaning a stable! That makes me hope my premonition is wrong."

"Hercules did it with a river, I think. But of course you'd probably have to use—"

"Please don't say a pitchfork," Herculeah interrupted.

"I wasn't going to," Meat lied.

Herculeah smiled and yawned. "Meat, I've got to hang up. I can't hold my eyes open. I'm falling asleep."

"Oh, well, all right," Meat said with reluctance. "Good night, Herculeah."

"Good night, Meat."

Herculeah put the phone down and turned off the light. "Cleaning a stable," she said, as she closed her eyes. "Yuck."

And from his stand, Tarot fluttered his wings and screeched, "Beware!"

What's in store for Herculeah?

Don't miss her next
terrifying adventure,

DEAD LETTER

When Herculeah Jones discovers a letter in her secondhand coat, she instantly recognizes it as a cry for help. Who wrote the letter, and what happened to them? It doesn't take Herculeah long to uncover the clues and track down the truth. But what Herculeah doesn't realize is that someone is stalking her—someone who would kill to keep the truth under wraps....